THE MARK OF

Isobel Grace

SHONDA TERRILL

ISBN:

979-8-9953803-0-6 (Paperback)

Published by Midnight Ink Press

Cover design by Midnight Ink Press

Dedication

For my dad, who I am more like than either of us will admit.

For my mother, whose love shaped me.

For my grandmothers, whose love never wavered.

For my sister — smart as hell and still a pain in my ass, but I love her so much.

For Todd, my best friend, who never stops showing up.

For Reuel, whose belief and support made this possible.

And for my children — my heart, my magic, my always.

Table of Contents

Chapter
- 1 -
The Awakening

After getting the girls on the bus, still half asleep, I hit the button on the coffee pot and sit on a barstool waiting for what feels like eternity for the divine cup of caffeine that keeps me functioning.

My phone rings, startling me. I just stare at it.

That distinctive ringtone — "The Devil Went Down to Georgia."

My head spins while I debate whether I should even answer.

It's him.

Every time he calls, it turns into an argument. It's never just a simple conversation.

Ugh. I really don't feel like doing this right now.

I answer anyway.

"Hello."

"Oh. Hey, Matt. What's up?"

I make sure my voice sounds as tired as I feel, letting him know the call isn't welcome.

"Hey, Izzy. I wanted to talk to you about getting the girls for a month this summer."

"No!"

The word flies out of my mouth before I can even think.

Here comes the word vomit I can't seem to control when it comes to him.

I begin pacing, rage building fast. "Matt, you never call them. You work crazy hours. I'm not letting you have them so they can sit home alone while you're working. They're twelve and fifteen. They are not old enough to be alone all day."

"Izzy, you need to trust me. Samantha moved in. She can watch them."

I let out a sharp laugh.

"Oh sure, Matt. Your teenage girlfriend would be a great babysitter for my children. Oh wait — she was our babysitter. I forgot." He can definitely hear the sarcasm in my voice. "Have you lost your fucking mind?"

"Final answer. No."

I hang up before he can respond.

My blood is boiling.

How could he even ask that? He didn't even ask to see them when we lived in the same damn town five minutes away from each other.

My anger keeps climbing. My face feels hot. Ugh, is this anger or a hot flash? My hands tremble, and the tips of my fingers burn.

The tears are right there.

I hate that man.

I truly fucking hate him.

The air in the room tightens.

I toss my phone onto the kitchen island, not caring if it breaks. I rest my elbows on the counter and bury my face in my hands.

I am not going to let this man make me cry. Not anymore.

For a split second, I think maybe a small break from the kids wouldn't be the worst thing in the world.

Then guilt slams into me just as fast.

My ears perk up.

What is that sound?

A rattle.

I turn toward the cabinets.

The one that holds my coffee cups and glasses is shaking.

What the fuck is going on? I know this house is old, but what the hell?

I walk toward it slowly.

I need a coffee cup anyway.

I reach for the cabinet handle, layered thick with years of paint. The glass panels have probably been replaced more than once.

I grab the knob.

Bam.

The cabinet explodes.

Coffee cups and glasses shoot out like they've been fired from a cannon. Glass shatters against the opposite cabinets, splintering across the tile. A mug slams into the wall and bursts into pieces before it ever hits the floor.

I barely move in time.

Another cup smashes into the center island, knocking over the fruit basket.

Fruit goes airborne.

An orange rockets through the kitchen window, shattering the glass. Bananas, kiwis, apples — everything is flying. Glass ricochets off cabinet doors. Something crashes against the refrigerator. The sound is deafening.

My kitchen is being torn apart.

I drop to the floor.

What in the actual fuck is happening right now?

I scramble into the corner, tears streaming down my face. I have never been this scared in my life. My hands cover my head. My face buries into my knees. I force myself to look up just enough to see the chaos around me.

Am I going to die right now?

And then—

Silence.

Complete silence.

I stay there for a full minute, maybe longer.

When I finally stand, my kitchen is destroyed.

Glass everywhere.

Fruit smashed.

Debris covering the floor.

But the island—

The island is clear.

No glass.

No fruit.

No wreckage.

Just one coffee cup.

The one I was reaching for.

It stands balanced on its bottom edge, slightly tilted.

Impossible.

This defies physics.

I glance at the clock.

7:34 a.m.

I crouch down until I'm eye level with it.

It does not tremble.

It does not shake.

It does not move.

I slowly walk around the island.

Still nothing.

It feels like forever.

I check the clock again.

7:37 a.m.

Three minutes.

Three full minutes, and it hasn't fallen.

Not a tremble. Not a breath of movement.

Then—

DING.

My heart nearly stops.

It's just the coffee maker telling me the coffee is ready.

I circle the island one more time before reaching for the handle.

The cup trembles slightly under my fingers.

I freeze.

It doesn't fall.

I wrap my hand around it and lift it easily, like gravity suddenly remembered its job.

I walk to the coffee pot and pour a cup.

I lean against the counter, the warmth of the morning sun pressing against my back through the window.

The house is quiet again.

Too quiet.

After all that crazy shit, I feel something else rising inside me.

Not fear.

Not rage.

Power.

I don't know what the hell this is.

But I'm sure as shit going to find out.

Chapter
- 2 -
The Mark

The clock says 8:12 a.m.

My kitchen looks like a damn war zone.

Glass everywhere. Fruit smashed into the tile like a toddler had a meltdown. The window over the sink stands wide open where that rogue orange decided to test its freedom.

For a moment, I just stand there.

Then it hits me like a ton of bricks.

The girls.

Shit.

They'll be home by 3:45.

They cannot walk into this.

I have to clean this shit up. Now.

Trash bag first. Then broom. Then towels. I don't think. I don't analyze. I just move.

Glass scrapes across the floor in long, sharp lines. Every time my brain replays Matt's voice — Samantha moved in — my grip tightens on the broom.

That stupid bitch.

A home-wrecking bitch.

The broom hits harder against the tile.

A cabinet creaks behind me.

I freeze.

Silence.

"It's just the house, Izzy," I say too myself. "It's old. It creaks. It makes creepy sounds."

I shake my head. Stress. That's all this is. Stress, lack of sleep, and hormones trying to kill me from the inside out.

I turn on music. Loud.

Something from high school. Something reckless. Familiar.

I may have been raised a country girl, but I still love me some Metallica.

The sound fills the kitchen, drowning out the echo of shattering glass still replaying in my head.

I move faster.

Sweep.

Bag.

Wipe.

I drag the step stool over and inspect the cabinet. The hinges are intact. No cracks in the wood. No splintering.

How in the hell is that possible?

Nothing that explains why it decided to launch my dishware like it was auditioning for a hurricane.

"This makes zero fucking sense," I say out loud.

At the sink, I rinse off a surviving plate, letting the water run longer than necessary.

Sunlight spills through the broken window and catches the back of my hand.

For a split second—

Something flashes.

Metallic.

Gold. Maybe purple.

I jerk my hand back.

Nothing.

Just skin.

I lean closer.

Still nothing.

"Great. I'm fucking hallucinating now."

"Get it together, Izzy," I say.

The water in the sink ripples once.

I turn it off immediately.

Silence.

By noon, the glass is gone. The fruit is history. I dig out the extra box of cups I never unpacked and shove them into the cabinet like they've always lived there.

Problem solved.

Right?

I lean on the broom, letting Metallica blast through the kitchen while I try not to think about floating coffee cups.

The singer hits the chorus—

The sound cuts.

Mid-lyric.

No fade.

No warning.

Just gone.

The silence is deafening.

My thoughts rush in all at once — the cabinet exploding, the balanced cup, the shimmer on my hand.

Before I can spiral—

The kitchen windows swing open.

Both of them.

Not slamming. Not violent. Just a firm push outward.

Warm air rushes in, lifting the curtains.

My fingers start to tingle again.

Not burning like they did when I was talking to Matt.

Warm.

Alive.

I don't move.

I don't step back.

I lean lightly on the broom and watch.

A shard of glass slides out from beneath the refrigerator.

Slow.

Deliberate.

"You've got to be kidding me."

It scrapes across the tile until it stops in front of the trash can.

There's a pause.

Then it lifts.

Parallel to the trash can lid.

Drops neatly inside.

The lid flips once.

Twice.

Then keeps spinning lazily in slow circles before finally settling closed.

The breeze stops as suddenly as it started.

The windows remain open, but the air goes still.

I stare at the trash can.

"What the hell…"

But I'm not scared.

A slow smile pulls at the corner of my mouth.

"Okay," I say quietly. "So that's how we're doing this now?"

My fingers cool gradually, the warmth settling back under my skin.

At 3:27 p.m., I'm standing at the sink pretending none of it happened.

The front door bursts open.

"Mom!" the girls yell.

Backpacks drop. Shoes kick off. Laughter fills the hallway.

They don't notice the new cups in the cabinet.

They don't ask about the window.

They don't see anything strange at all.

Nothing.

I watch them for a moment.

Normal.

Safe.

Untouched.

I glance down at my hand.

Nothing there.

Just skin.

But I can still feel it.

And this time—

I'm not afraid.

Chapter
- 3 -
Pages

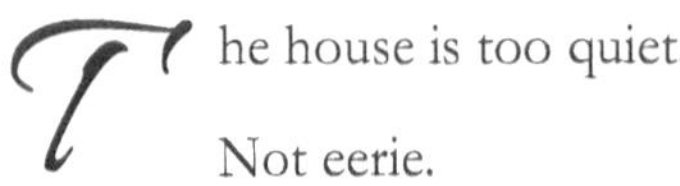

The house is too quiet.

Not eerie.

Just … aware.

The girls are at school. The dishes are done. The kitchen looks normal again, like it didn't try to rearrange itself yesterday. I keep trying not to think about that tornado, but the flashes keep coming.

I stand at the bottom of the attic ladder longer than I need to. The handle is coated in dust.

It's been years since anyone's been up here.

Hopefully, it's empty.

Mom lived here, too — not just Grandma Dorothy. Maybe she left something behind.

I always miss her. Most of my memories are intact, but they feel fragile, like photographs handled too often.

Mom was beautiful. Long, blonde hair that caught the light. My brown, ruddy hair came from Dad.

"Thanks, Dad," I say.

I tell myself I'm just checking for damage. That's all.

Making sure nothing else decides to launch itself across the room.

My back aches after hours of cleaning. Getting older is not for the faint of heart.

I look up and reach for the cord without thinking twice.

The ladder creaks as it unfolds.

"Relax," I chastise — not sure if I'm talking to the house or myself.

Warm air hits my face as I climb. The attic smells like dust, cedar, and summers I remember clearly.

Sunlight filters through the small, circular window at the far end, catching particles in the air like suspended glitter.

Boxes line the walls.

Neat.

Labeled.

Grandma's handwriting is unmistakable — tight, clean, deliberate. Nothing wasted.

I climb fully into the attic and pause.

She was never as scattered as people thought. This place is organized. Intentional.

One cedar trunk sits near the center beam.

Not shoved aside or forgotten.

Placed.

It belongs there.

I kneel in front of it.

The metal latch is cool against my fingers.

Then it happens again.

That warmth.

Not the sharp, protective heat from the kitchen.

Something softer.

Something deeper.

It spreads through my fingertips and into my palm — steady and familiar.

Not a warning.

A welcome.

Images rush through me: Mom laughing, Grandma standing at the stove, the feeling of being small and safe and watched over. The warmth grows, wrapping around me like memory made physical.

For a second, I hesitate.

Then, I lift the latch.

The trunk creaks open.

Inside are journals.

Stacked carefully. Edges worn. Leather softened by years of use.

These weren't decorative.

They were lived in.

I pick up the top one. The leather bends easily beneath my fingers, supple from being opened and closed hundreds — maybe thousands — of times.

A cord wraps around it. An old-fashioned key dangles from the end.

I test it in the trunk's lock. It fits.

Click.

A small, absurd spark of satisfaction flickers through me.

The first page is dated:

September 1, 1990.

To me, 1990 feels like yesterday. To my kids, it's ancient history.

Her handwriting fills the page — steady, deliberate, commanding attention.

Not rambling.

Not mystical nonsense.

Precise.

I flip forward.

Another entry.

Another date.

Careful record keeping.

Not madness.

My throat tightens.

I turn to a random page and read.

If you are reading this, then you have come home.

I stare at the sentence.

The air shifts.

Not threatening.

Grounded.

I keep reading.

The line passes through the women. It always has.

Your mother was ready at eighteen.

You were not here to be told.

I stop breathing.

I turn the page.

The law is not punishment. It is protection.

The mark reveals itself when the circle is nearby.

Blood recognizes blood.

Me?

Is she talking about me?

I flip forward frantically, but a sudden pressure flattens the pages back to the original entry.

Your mother was ready at eighteen.

You were not here to be told.

"I didn't know," I whisper, like she might answer.

My fingers tingle faintly.

I close the journal halfway.

"This is insane," I say out loud.

But I don't put it down.

I flip further.

References to rituals — without detail.

Gatherings.

Women.

A line drawn between above and below.

And then—

Blank pages.

Waiting.

A chill runs through me.

Not fear.

Recognition.

I close the journal and sit back on my heels.

The attic is silent.

No creaking.

No shifting.

Just stillness.

I glance down at my hand.

For a moment — longer than before — a faint metallic sheen rests beneath my skin.

Not bright.

Not glowing.

Present.

I don't jerk away.

I just watch.

"Okay," I say softly.

The shimmer fades.

The attic remains still.

Since the cabinets exploded in my kitchen—

I don't feel crazy.

I don't feel afraid.

I feel aligned.

Like something has been waiting.

And I've finally arrived.

Chapter
- 4 -
I am Isobel Grace

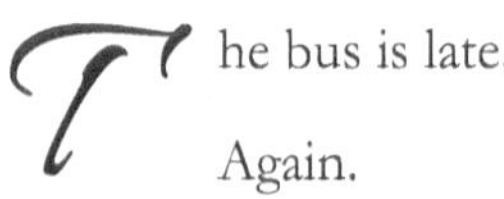

he bus is late.

Again.

My fifteen-year-old, Lily, is leaning against the porch rail like she pays bills here, thumb scrolling like the world might end if she looks up for three seconds.

My twelve-year-old, Rose, is humming under her breath — that low, irritated tune she does when she's about to combust.

I check my watch.

Then the street.

Then my watch again like that'll magically summon the yellow miracle and save me from the nightmare shit show that is the school drop-off line.

Nothing.

"Are you kidding me?" I say.

The bus rounds the corner.

And keeps going.

"Oh, for the love of God—" I drag my hands down my face. "Y'all missed the damn bus."

"Mom!" Rose gasps. "Language!"

"Sorry," I say flatly.

Lily smirks. "A little dramatic there before coffee, Mom?"

"Okay." I clap once. "New plan. Get in the car, my little crotch goblins. I'm driving."

They groan in unison.

"Don't 'ugh' me," I shoot back, grabbing my keys. "I'm the reason you have snacks, cellphones, and Wi-Fi."

Rose laughs. Lily rolls her eyes like she's practicing for a future career in a teenage drama TV series.

"Shoes. Hair. Backpack. Move," I say, and they scatter like Texas cockroaches when you flip on the lights

The ride is loud for exactly thirty seconds.

"Mom, she's touching me!" Rose yells.

"I did not touch you, drama queen," Lily says.

"Do not make me pull this car over," I warn. "We are playing the quiet game. Starting now."

Green Day hums through the speakers. Silence follows.

Finally.

I try not to think about the tornado that happened two days ago in my kitchen. Like that bitch might throw hands again and attack me. The cabinets deciding

they hate

me. The way my body felt — hot, protective, not mine — like something inside me woke up and chose violence.

Not today.

Today is normal.

Today is drop-off day, like real moms do.

Today is me pretending I'm not one weird breeze away from becoming the neighborhood legend.

We pull into the line.

Rose leans forward.

"Mom?"

"What?"

"You've been weird."

There it is.

I glance at her in the rearview mirror. Twelve going on twenty-five. Too observant for her own good.

"I'm fine," I say gently. "Just tired."

"You're always tired."

"Correct. That's what happens when you give birth to two adorable demons."

Rose laughs. Lily rolls her eyes but smiles anyway.

I give the standard speech.

"Be nice. Don't start fights. If you start a fight, win. Kidding. Mostly. And please, for the love of all things holy, don't pick your nose in public."

"Love you," says Rose, leaning in to kiss my cheek.

Lily squeezes my shoulder before hopping out.

They disappear into the school.

The car goes quiet.

Not peaceful.

Just … empty.

I look down at my hands on the steering wheel.

Normal hands.

No shimmer.

No heat.

No strange pulse under my skin.

Just the faint tan line where my wedding ring used to live.

Good.

Stay normal, Izzy.

I pull into a coffee shop parking lot because I have time before work, and my house has been feeling a little too … aware lately.

Like it might attack me.

Inside, the bulletin board is massive clutter: tutors, dog walkers, a chiropractor who looks like he could bench-press my emotional baggage

I pause.

Damn.

He's kinda hot.

My back does hurt.

I snap a picture.

Then I immediately think: that's photo number 14,382 that will live in my iCloud forever and never be seen again.

And then I see something.

A pale yellow sheet.

WOMEN'S CIRCLE — THURSDAYS 10 A.M.

Coffee. Conversation. No judgment.

New faces welcome.

There's a symbol at the bottom. Simple. A circle split clean through the middle.

I stare at it longer than I mean to.

Not because it's pretty.

Because something about it tugs.

Familiar.

Like a song I know but can't place.

"Women's circle," I say to no one. "That's either wholesome as hell or culty as shit."

I tear off the tab anyway.

Honestly?

It's got to be better than sitting alone in my kitchen waiting for my cabinets to try and murder my ass again, so I decide to head to it.

The meeting is in a community room behind the library. It smells like carpet cleaner, old paper, and slightly suppressed emotions.

Six women sit in a loose circle.

Heads turn when I walk in.

I'm wearing jeans, boots, and a black tee that says DON'T TEST ME.

Because I have a personality and I'm not hiding it.

"Hi," I say. "I'm Izzy. I saw your flyer and figured I'd come see if y'all are normal or if I'm about to get recruited into a pyramid scheme."

Beat.

Then laughter.

"Oh, thank God," a silver-haired woman says. "She's not a robot."

A blonde in a denim jacket points at the chair next to her. "Sit, Izzy. We do intros when someone new shows up. And we absolutely cuss. It's basically in the bylaws."

"Perfect," I say, taking the seat. "I cuss like a fucking sailor, so sounds like I will fit in just fine."

My shoulders relax.

Okay.

These are my people.

Introductions go around the circle.

JoAnne, fifty-four, divorced, two grown kids.

Emma, forty-eight, widowed, two boys.

Lucy, forty-nine, married, one grown daughter, but still fantasizes about cabin solitude.

Taylor, forty-nine, married, teen daughters, surviving driver's permits.

Maddie, forty-five, divorced, two girls — husband left her for his assistant.

And then—

Rowan.

Forty-seven. Single mom. Two kids — sixteen and thirteen.

Rowan has short, brown hair cut just below her jaw, practical and intentional. Not styled to soften her. Styled to say stay out of her way.

The kind of woman who knows where every exit is without turning her head.

"I'm here," Rowan says, "because life is loud. This makes it softer."

Our eyes meet for just a second too long.

Not dramatic.

Just steady.

Conversation rolls easy after that.

Perimenopause rage.

Target meltdowns.

Bras betraying us.

Kids calling us, "bruh."

I laugh harder than I have in days.

This feels normal.

This feels good.

JoAnne claps her hand loudly. "Alright ladies, reminder: next Saturday is our night out," she says. "We do it once a month, so we remember we're humans and not just chauffeurs with hot flashes, debt, and asshole kids."

When the meeting winds down, Rowan steps closer as chairs scrape against the floor.

"So," she says lightly, "Izzy. Is that short for anything?"

I pause.

Because it shouldn't matter.

But it does.

"My full name is…" I laugh softly. "God, I haven't said it in forever."

Her eyes don't leave mine.

Patient.

Certain.

"Isobel," I say. "Isobel Grace."

My grandmother was the only one who ever called me that.

Rowan smiles.

Small.

Intent.

"Isobel," she repeats. "That suits you."

Something flickers behind her eyes.

Not surprise.

Recognition.

Rowan reaches into her bag and pulls out her phone. "You seem like you'd be good people. Want to swap numbers? There's a coffee place down the street that doesn't serve burnt-ass espresso."

When her fingers brush mine, there's the faintest shock. Like static after walking across carpet in socks.

She notices.

Doesn't react.

Just smiles.

Before I can respond, Maddie drags a chair across the floor and drops into it backwards, arms folded over the backrest.

"What's this?" she asks, grinning. "Y'all planning secret meetings without me?"

"Just coffee," says Rowan, smoothly.

Maddie gasps dramatically. "Oh, absolutely not. I need coffee and adult interaction. I have a twelve-year-old and a twenty-one-year-old. I deserve this."

Rowan glances at me. "That work for you?"

I shrug. "The more the merrier."

"Done," says Maddie, pulling out her phone. "I'm inviting myself."

We exchange numbers.

It feels easy.

Normal.

Like we're just three tired women making plans.

"Text me," Rowan says. "We'll all grab coffee soon. I have Maddie's number."

As I step outside into the afternoon sun, everything looks the same.

Cars. Wind. Sirens in the distance.

Normal.

But my phone feels heavier in my pocket — in a good way.

And my name feels … returned.

Isobel.

Whatever this is—

I'm not walking away.

I'm walking closer.

Chapter
- 5 -
Proof

The coffee shop smells like espresso and cinnamon and other people's better decisions.

I get there five minutes early, which is not my brand, but apparently my nervous system is trying new hobbies.

I claim a table near the window, in the corner in case our conversation leads to cussing and loud laughter.

Not in the middle of the room. Close enough to feel normal. Far enough to feel safe.

My phone sits beside my cup like it's heavier than it should be.

Two numbers.

Two women.

One weird name I haven't said out loud in years. My name.

Isobel.

I take a sip and immediately regret it because it tastes like burnt ambition.

I glance at the door again.

Relax, Izzy.

You're meeting moms. For coffee.

Not negotiating a hostage situation or planning a murder. I chuckle a little.

Still … my stomach won't listen.

The bell over the door jingles, and Maddie walks in like she belongs everywhere she goes — bright scarf, pink hair, big energy, and a smile that says she's survived worse than this room.

She spots me, waves, and slides into the chair across from me like we've been friends for years.

"Okay," she says, setting her coffee down. "First things first. This place is cute, but if this espresso tastes like regret, I'm suing."

I snort. "Please do. I'll testify."

Maddie grins. "How are the kids today? Have a good morning?"

"Barely," I say. "They missed the damn bus again, so I got promoted to full-time chauffeur before coffee."

I add, "Rose doing this humming thing she does. Lily ignoring the world, her phone is all that matters."

"Ah." Maddie nods solemnly. "The hum. The hum is always the beginning of the end."

I laugh, and it loosens something in my chest.

There. That's why I came. That feeling. Like I'm not the only adult losing her damn mind in silence.

The bell jingles again.

Rowan steps inside.

She moves differently than Maddie. Quieter. Slower. Like the room makes space for her without realizing it.

Jeans, boots, simple top. No performance. No fuss.

She sees me and gives a small smile that doesn't ask for anything.

She walks over and sits down beside Maddie, angled slightly toward me.

"Hi," she says.

"Hi," I answer, and my voice comes out softer than I mean it to.

Maddie leans back like she's settling in for a show. "Okay. A trio. I like this. I feel like we should have a group name."

"Absolutely not," I say. "I refuse to be in a named group."

Maddie squints. "That's exactly what someone in a named group would say."

Rowan's mouth twitches like she's trying not to smile.

She lifts her cup, takes a sip, and looks at me over the rim.

No rush.

No pressure.

Just … present.

The silence that follows isn't awkward.

It's intentional.

Maddie clears her throat loudly. "So, Izzy. Tell us something fun. Like … what's your toxic trait."

I blink. "I'm sorry?"

Maddie gestures vaguely. "Like, mine is that I think I can fix anyone, and then I get mad when they don't fix themselves after I tell them how to do it."

I stare at her.

Then laugh. "Okay. Mine is that I pretend I'm fine until I'm not, and then I say something unhinged like 'my house is aware' and scare everyone."

Maddie's eyes light up. "Oh, I love that one."

Rowan sets her cup down gently.

"Does your house feel aware?" she asks, casually as if she's asking about the weather.

My laugh dies halfway.

My fingers tighten around my cup.

Maddie keeps her face neutral, but she doesn't look surprised.

I glance back and forth between them.

"Why are you asking me that?" I say, trying to sound like I'm joking, but it comes out too sharp.

Rowan doesn't flinch.

"Because you said it the other day," she replies. "And because you looked like you were holding something in."

I swallow.

"It's not, um, I mean I'm not—" I start, then stop.

Because what am I even doing?

Pretending this is normal?

Pretending my kitchen didn't try to kill me?

Pretending my grandmother didn't leave journals that read like a warning label for my life?

I set the cup down, so my hand doesn't shake.

"I've been … weird," I admit. "Rose even told me I've been weird lately."

I shrug slightly.

Maddie nods like I just told her I'm tired.

Rowan's gaze stays steady.

"What happened?" Rowan asks.

I stare at the table. The wood grain. The sugar packets. The tiny scuffs.

Normal things.

Safe things.

"My cabinets," I say finally. "They—" I exhale. "They flew open. Like … violently. Like something was angry. I think my house may be haunted. I don't know."

I hear myself and want to crawl under the table.

Rowan doesn't react.

Maddie doesn't blink.

I keep going because now it's out and I can't shove it back in.

"And then my hand … it did this thing. Like heat, but not pain. Like … power. That sounds nuts. I know it sounds crazy."

Rowan tilts her head. "Did you get hurt?"

"No," I say quickly. "No. It was like … it stopped before it could. Like it was warning me. I know y'all both think I sound mental right now."

Maddie exhales through her nose, almost laughing. "Okay, yeah. That tracks."

I look at her. "That tracks?"

Maddie lifts her cup and sips like we're talking about the weather.

Rowan's voice stays calm. "How long has this been happening?"

"It hasn't," I say. "Not like that. Not until—" I stop myself.

Not until Grandma's house.

Not until the attic.

Not until the journal.

My throat tightens.

Rowan watches me very carefully.

"Have you found anything up there?" she asks.

"In the attic?" I blurt, then immediately regret it.

Rowan doesn't look impressed that she guessed it. She just nods once.

Maddie's eyes flick to Rowan for half a second — quick, silent communication — then back to me.

I don't know what I'm stepping into, but I feel it.

A door.

A line.

A choice.

"Yes," I say quietly. "Journals."

Rowan's fingers rest on the table, relaxed. Nothing about her is tense, and that almost makes it worse.

Because she looks like she already knew.

My pulse stutters.

I force a laugh, thin and ugly. "This is the part where you both tell me I need sleep and therapy, right?"

Maddie's expression softens.

"Girl, everybody's fucked up. Therapy's just maintenance."

Rowan says nothing.

She glances at the sugar caddy sitting in the center of the table.

Just a simple white container with packets sticking out like little flags.

She looks back up at me.

And then she reaches out her hand — not dramatic, not theatrical — palm open, fingers relaxed, like she's just going to take one.

The sugar caddy shifts.

Not flying.

Not sliding across the table like a magic trick.

Just … moving.

Two inches.

Quiet.

Smooth.

As if the table itself decided to help her.

It settles against her fingertips.

Rowan picks up a packet between her fingers like she moved it with nothing but habit.

My breath catches.

I stare at the sugar.

I stare at her hand.

I stare at the space it crossed.

No one in the coffee shop reacts.

No one looks over.

No barista screams.

No one drops a cup.

The world keeps spinning.

My brain doesn't.

Rowan shakes the packet, tears it open, and pours it into her cup like she didn't just tilt my entire reality by two inches.

Then she looks at me.

"You're not crazy," she says softly.

My throat tightens.

I blink fast, like that might undo what I just saw.

I laugh once — small, shaky. "That—" I swallow. "That was … what the hell was that?"

Rowan's voice stays even. "Proof."

Maddie finally sets her cup down.

She doesn't look at the sugar.

She looks at me.

"I thought I was losing my damn mind at first," she says, like she once bled through low-rise jeans in middle school. "Like, actual 'check myself into a facility' levels."

I stare at her. "You, too?"

Maddie nods. "Oh, honey. Yes, bless your little heart."

Rowan's gaze doesn't soften, but it doesn't harden either.

It's steady.

Safe.

Like a hand on the back of your shirt when you're about to step off a ledge.

My voice comes out thin. "So … what am I?"

Rowan pauses, just long enough to show she's choosing her words.

Then she says, gently, "You're waking up."

My pulse thumps.

My skin prickles.

My stomach flips.

I should be terrified.

But all I feel is relief so sharp it burns.

Because I'm not insane.

I'm not alone.

I'm late.

But I'm here.

Rowan leans in slightly, lowering her voice as if the air itself might listen.

"Tell me," she says, "when did it start?"

And for the first time since the kitchen, I don't try to joke it away.

I don't try to swallow it.

I just breathe.

"Start at the beginning," she says. "And don't leave anything out."

Rowan's expression doesn't change.

And somehow, that's what scares me most.

Chapter
- 6 -
Waking Up

or a long moment, no one speaks.

The café hums around us — milk steaming, chairs scraping, someone laughing too loudly near the door — but it feels distant.

Like I'm underwater.

Rowan's fingers rest lightly around her coffee cup. Maddie watches me, not worried, not urgent.

Just steady.

"You're waking up," Rowan says.

I swallow. "Okay," I manage. "Let's say I believe you."

My voice sounds thin to my own ears.

"Let's say I'm not losing my mind."

Rowan nods once.

"Then what does that mean?"

Maddie exhales softly, almost amused. "It means welcome to the weird side."

Rowan doesn't smile. She studies me instead.

"It means," she says carefully, "you're beginning to feel what's always been there."

The words drop in my chest like a weight I didn't know I was carrying.

I shake my head. "No. That's not possible. I would've known."

Rowan's gaze shifts, just slightly.

"Would you?"

Something in her tone makes me sit straighter.

I hesitate, then the question pushes out of me before I can stop it.

"How did you know my grandmother?"

There it is.

The thing that's been crawling under my skin since yesterday.

Rowan doesn't look surprised I asked.

She leans back slightly in her chair, eyes thoughtful.

"I grew up around her," she says.

The words are simple.

But they change everything.

I stare at her. "You knew her?"

"Yes."

My heart pounds once, hard.

"She never mentioned you."

A faint smile touches Rowan's mouth.

"She wouldn't have."

That unsettles me more than the sugar sliding across the table.

"Why not?"

Rowan glances down at the table for a second, then back at me.

"She believed you should live your life without … pressure."

Pressure.

I laugh softly. "She didn't tell me anything. I didn't even know she was sick until it was almost over."

Maddie's eyes soften.

Rowan nods.

"She didn't want to pull you back," she says.

"Back to what?"

Rowan tilts her head slightly.

"Back to here."

The word settles between us.

Here.

The house.

The land.

Whatever this is.

I swallow.

"She died when I was twenty-two," I say quietly. "I was married, raising kids. I was … distracted."

I don't add the rest.

Young.

Naïve.

In love with the wrong man.

Rowan's voice stays calm.

"She knew she wouldn't be here when it started."

My breath catches.

"When what started?"

She holds my gaze.

"This."

A chill runs down my spine — not fear.

Recognition.

"She wrote journals," I say. "Pages and pages. Like she was documenting something. Waiting for something."

Rowan nods again.

"She was."

"For what?" I press.

"For you to come back."

The words don't feel dramatic.

They feel inevitable.

I stare at her.

"You're telling me she expected this?"

"She hoped," Rowan corrects gently. "There's a difference."

My pulse steadies, strangely.

"She never told me any of this."

"She didn't need to."

I let out a short, breathless laugh. "That's not comforting."

Rowan's expression softens just a fraction.

"She believed if it was yours, it would find you, or you would find it."

My mind flickers back to the attic.

The trunk.

The key.

The line in the journal.

If you are reading this, then you have come home.

My throat tightens.

"You knew she was dying," I say.

It's not an accusation.

It's a realization.

Rowan nods slowly.

"Yes."

"Did she … did she say anything about me?"

Maddie looks down at her cup, giving us space.

Rowan considers the question carefully, like it deserves precision.

"She said you had your own path," she says. "And that you would choose it."

I frown. "Choose what?"

Rowan's eyes flick briefly to my hands.

"Whether to step into this," she says quietly.

I glance down.

My fingers are steady.

No shimmer.

No heat.

But I feel something there.

Waiting.

"She left me the house because I'm her last relative," I say, trying to anchor myself in something practical.

"Yes," Rowan agrees.

"That doesn't mean I'm … whatever this is."

"No," she says evenly. "It doesn't."

The relief that hits me surprises me.

"So, this isn't some bloodline crown situation?" I ask dryly.

Maddie snorts into her coffee.

Rowan's mouth curves slightly.

"No crowns," she says. "No automatic rank."

I exhale slowly.

"Good. I don't look good in tiaras."

Maddie lifts her cup. "Speak for yourself."

But Rowan's gaze stays serious.

"Power runs through families," she says. "But what you do with it — how far you go — that's not inherited. That's cultivated."

I absorb that.

"So, she wasn't just … eccentric."

Rowan's expression shifts.

"She carried responsibility," says Rowan, instead. "She protected more than people realized."

Protected.

The word seems fitting when it comes to Grandma.

"Protected what?" I ask.

Rowan pauses.

Not avoiding.

Choosing.

"You'll understand that soon enough."

I narrow my eyes. "That's not an answer."

"It's the one I can give you today."

Maddie leans forward slightly.

"You don't have to decide anything right now," she says gently. "You just have to pay attention."

"To what?"

Rowan answers this time.

"To what responds to you."

Silence settles again.

But it's different now.

Not empty.

Charged.

I think about the cabinets flying open.

The heat in my hands.

The journals.

The symbol on the flyer.

The weird mark on my hand.

The way my name felt when Rowan said it.

Isobel.

"She thought I'd come back," I say slowly.

Rowan nods once and speaks.

"She believed you would."

"And if I hadn't?"

Rowan's gaze doesn't waver.

"Then it would have waited."

The certainty in her voice makes my skin prickle.

I don't feel chosen.

I don't feel special.

I fee l… responsible.

Not to them.

To something older.

I sit back in my chair.

"So, what happens now?"

Rowan studies me for a long beat.

Then she says, calmly,

"Now you decide how much you want to know."

And the strangest thing is —

I don't hesitate.

"I want all of it," I say.

Maddie smiles.

Rowan's expression doesn't change.

But something in her eyes settles.

"Good," she says softly.

"Then we'll start. But you need to understand something first — this doesn't undo."

I don't hesitate.

"Good."

Chapter
- 7 -
Control

The house is quiet.

Not the tense kind of quiet.

Just a quiet morning.

Backpacks gone. Shoes by the door. The faint smell of toast hanging in the air.

The girls are at school.

It's just me. Isobel. My name still feels heavy when I say it.

Sunlight spills across the kitchen counter in long golden strips, catching dust in the air like tiny floating secrets.

I pour my coffee slowly.

No cabinet explosions.

No violent wind that doesn't exist.

Just the hum of the refrigerator and the steady drip of the machine.

Normal.

I wrap my fingers around the mug and lean back against the counter.

Rowan's hand.

The sugar.

Two inches.

Not dramatic.

Not loud.

Deliberate.

I set my coffee down.

"If this is real," I murmur softly to the empty kitchen, "then I want to do it on purpose."

No anger.

No fear.

Just intention.

I reach into the drawer and pull out a teaspoon.

It clinks lightly against the counter as I set it down flat, right in the center of the sunlight.

I don't rush.

I place it exactly where I want it.

Like I'm setting a boundary.

I inhale.

Slow.

I exhale.

Slower.

I remember the kitchen the other day — the heat, the explosion, the loss of control, when I thought the house was out for blood.

That wasn't this.

This feels different.

This feels like stepping toward something instead of reacting to it.

I straighten slightly.

Not forcing.

Inviting.

"Move," I whisper.

Nothing happens.

I almost laugh at myself.

Forty-seven years old and talking to a damn spoon!

I close my eyes.

Breathe again.

Calm.

Focus.

Not reaching out with my hands.

Reaching inward.

There's something there.

Low.

Warm.

Like an ember that's been waiting for oxygen.

I don't push it.

I let it rise.

When I open my eyes, the spoon is exactly where I left it.

Of course it didn't move.

Fantastic. I've officially lost my mind before lunch.

My mouth twitches.

"Okay," I say. "That was anticlimactic."

I focus again.

Not harder.

Just clearer.

I don't picture it flying.

I picture it sliding.

Just a little.

Two inches.

Like the sugar.

The air feels thicker.

Not heavy.

Aware.

My pulse slows instead of racing.

That's new.

And then—

It moves.

Barely.

A tremor.

So slight I almost convince myself I imagined it.

I freeze.

My breath catches in my throat.

The spoon shifts again.

A soft metallic whisper against the stone countertop.

One inch.

Clean.

Controlled.

It stops right at my fingertips.

I stare at it and the space it crossed.

At the proof sitting in my kitchen like it belongs there.

No cabinets slam.

No windows rattle.

Nothing breaks.

It just … listens.

A slow smile spreads across my face.

Not wild.

Not manic.

Certain.

"Okay," I whisper.

I don't try to make it do more.

I don't test it.

I don't push.

I let the moment sit.

Let it settle into my bones.

Then, I reach for my phone.

My fingers hover for half a second before I type.

It moved.

I stare at the screen.

Three dots appear almost immediately.

Rowan: I know. I hoped you would try.

That's it.

No emojis.

No exclamation points.

No surprise.

Just knowing.

A chill runs through me — not fear though.

Recognition.

She felt it.

Or she expected it.

Or she's been waiting for it.

I press my lips together to keep from smiling too wide.

Then I scroll to Maddie's name.

Because I cannot sit in this alone.

The phone rings twice before she answers.

"Well, if it isn't my favorite almost-psychiatric-admit friend—"

She answers like we've been best friends for years.

"It moved," I blurt.

There's a beat of silence.

Then—

"Shut up."

"I swear to God, Maddie. A spoon. I put it on the counter. I breathed. I didn't freak out. And it moved."

"How far?" she demands.

"Like … an inch. Maybe a little more."

"Was anything destroyed?"

"No."

"Did anything explode?"

"No."

"Did you scream?"

"Only internally."

Maddie lets out a laugh that's half proud, half unhinged joy.

"Oh my God. Oh my God. I love this for you."

I laugh too, the sound bubbling up out of me before I can stop it.

"I didn't even get mad," I say. "I was calm. I was focused."

"Yes," she says immediately.

"When you're angry, it blows out. When you're steady, it obeys. You didn't blast it. You directed it."

Directed it.

The word lands deep.

I look back at the spoon.

Still resting in its new place.

Obedient.

Patient.

"It felt…" I hesitate. "Familiar."

Maddie goes quiet for a second.

"Yeah," she says softly. "That's because it is."

I lean against the counter again; phone pressed to my ear.

Sunlight still cuts across the kitchen.

My kitchen.

Not haunted.

Not angry.

Waiting.

"I'm not scared," I admit.

"Good," Maddie replies. "You shouldn't be."

I end the call a few minutes later, still smiling.

The house feels different now.

Not threatening.

Responsive.

I walk over and pick up the spoon, turning it slowly between my fingers.

"You and I," I say, "we're going to figure this out."

I set it back down.

Not as a test.

As a promise.

Upstairs, the attic door sits closed.

Quiet.

But no longer intimidating.

For the first time since I opened that trunk, I don't feel like something has found me.

I feel like I found it.

And this time—

I'm not reacting.

I'm reaching.

Chapter
- 8 -
The Lesson

Rowan's address leads me off the main road and into a neighborhood that looks like it forgot what year it is.

Live oaks lean over the street like old women gossiping. Moss hangs in soft curtains. The houses sit back from the road, polite and quaint, porches deep enough to hide secrets.

Rowan's place is at the end of a curved drive, tucked behind a wrought-iron gate that isn't locked.

Of course it isn't.

Her house is small-ish, one story, painted a color that can't decide if it's gray or green. The yard is tidy but not manicured— wild in the places it wants to be. Lavender spills over a border. Rosemary climbs like it owns the home. A wind chime taps gently somewhere, and the sound makes my skin prickle, like the air is paying attention.

I turn the engine off and sit there with my hands on the wheel for a beat longer than necessary.

The spoon.

The text.

Rowan: I know. I hoped you would try.

I still don't understand how a person can sound that calm through a phone screen.

I get out of the car, and the moment my feet hit the gravel, the front door opens.

Rowan is standing there like she's been waiting all morning— not in a robe, not dramatic, not holding a crystal ball or chanting into the wind.

She's wearing jeans and a soft black sweater, hair pulled back. No jewelry except a thin silver ring on her index finger.

Her eyes flick to my face, then to my hands, then briefly to my throat, like she's reading something I can't see.

"Come in," she says.

No greeting. No small talk. Just direction.

I follow her up the steps.

The inside of her house smells like dried herbs and lavender, too.

Witchy, yes— but clean witchy.

Organized witchy.

A place where you could brew something powerful and still find your keys.

Bundles of herbs hang from a ceiling rack like upside-down bouquets: sage, thyme, something darker and sharper I can't name. Glass jars line the shelves—roots, petals, powders—each labeled in neat handwriting. A long table sits against one wall with books stacked in careful piles, some leather-bound and cracked with age, others newer with dog-eared pages and sticky notes.

Cats are everywhere.

Not in an overwhelming way.

In a "we live here and you're visiting" way.

One black cat is sprawled across the back of a chair like it's posing for a painting. Another, gray and white, circles my ankles once, and then, ignores me completely.

Rowan shuts the door and turns.

"Did you bring it?" she asks.

"The spoon?" I say, because apparently this is my life now.

Her mouth twitches, just barely. "No. The journal."

I blink. "Oh."

I pull my bag higher on my shoulder. "Yes."

"Good," she says, as if she already knew the answer.

She gestures down the hall. "Kitchen."

Of course, it's the kitchen.

Every important thing in my life seems to be happening in kitchens lately.

Her kitchen is larger than mine and serene— not because it's empty, but because everything has a place. Copper pots hang neatly. A bundle of dried chili peppers is tied beside a wreath of garlic. A crock of wooden spoons sits beside a mortar and pestle worn smooth from use.

Rowan moves like she knows exactly where the air is thick and where it isn't.

She sets a candle on the table, sweeps her right hand over the wick, and it lights with one smooth motion.

The flame steadies immediately. No flicker. No drama.

Then she places a small glass of water beside it.

"I'm going to show you three things," she says. "Control. Containment. Cost."

I swallow. "Okay."

She doesn't ask if I'm ready.

Rowan slides a chair out for me, then sits across the table, hands folded, posture straight.

She looks like a teacher who doesn't tolerate nonsense.

"The spoon was a good first step," she says. "You did not force it. You asked."

I don't know why that makes me feel proud. It does anyway.

Rowan nods once, like she can see the reaction. "But control isn't about whether something moves."

She taps the table once, gently.

The candle flame doesn't even wobble.

"Control is whether you move."

My throat tightens. "I'm not—"

"Lie to yourself later," she says calmly. "Not here."

I shut my mouth.

"Lesson one," she says. "Fire."

She slides the dish toward me. The candle sits between us, flame steady, watching.

"Do not make it bigger," Rowan says. "Do not make it dance. Do not extinguish it."

"What do you want me to do?" I ask.

Rowan's gaze doesn't move from my face. "Hold it."

I stare at the flame.

It's so small. So normal.

And yet my palms start to sweat like I'm about to go on a first date.

I inhale slowly, like I did in my kitchen.

I exhale slower.

I don't reach with my hands.

I reach inward.

That warmth I felt before is there immediately, like it's been pacing behind a door, waiting for me to knock.

I let it rise. Not rushing. Not panicking.

I look at the candle flame, and I don't think it to move.

I think stay.

The flame steadies so completely it looks painted.

No tremor. No flutter.

Rowan's eyes narrow slightly.

I keep breathing.

Ten seconds.

Twenty.

Thirty.

The air around the table feels … aware.

Not heavy.

Present.

The cats have gone silent. Even their tails are still.

Rowan speaks softly, almost to herself. "Interesting."

My pulse tries to jump. I keep it down.

Finally, Rowan taps the table again. "That's enough."

I let the warmth sink back like a tide receding.

The flame flickers once—just once—then returns to normal.

I blink, realizing I was holding my breath.

Rowan studies me like she's looking for cracks. "How did it feel?"

I swallow. "Like … like holding a thought steady."

"Good," she says. "That's what it is."

She slides the glass of water toward me next. "Lesson two. Containment."

She dips her finger into the water and flicks three drops onto the wooden table.

The droplets sit there, perfect spheres.

"Don't touch them," she says. "Don't absorb them. Don't evaporate them."

"What do you want me to do?" I ask again.

Rowan's voice is patient in the way a sharp knife is patient. "Keep them where they are. That's all."

I stare at the droplets and suddenly I feel ridiculous.

And then I remember how ridiculous I felt talking to a spoon.

And then the spoon moved.

So.

I inhale.

Exhale.

Reach inward.

The warmth comes, steady now, like it recognizes the path.

I picture them staying.

Just staying.

The droplets tremble—just barely—and then they still.

Rowan watches without blinking.

A full minute passes.

Two.

The droplets don't spread. They don't soak in the wood.

They just … remain.

Rowan exhales once. "Most people can't do both on their first day."

"That's—"

"Don't," she says. "Don't make it small because you're afraid of what it means."

The words hit hard.

Rowan rests her palm on the journal.

"Lesson three," she says.

"Cost."

Rowan nods.

She pulls a thin string from her pocket and ties it loosely around her wrist.

"It's not a trick," she says. "It's a measure."

"A measure of what?"

"Of what happens when you don't contain it."

She leans in.

"You've been angry. Not just lately."

The warmth flares.

"You've swallowed things you shouldn't have swallowed. You've carried people who didn't deserve to be carried. You've been told you're too much and you believed it."

The candle flickers.

"Isobel," she says firmly. "Contain it."

"It's … pressure. Almost rage."

"Pressure is fine. Pressure is power waiting. Rage is what you need to contain."

The warmth surges.

"If you let it jump, it will jump. If you tell it to kneel—"

I inhale.

Exhale.

I picture kneeling.

And the warmth settles.

The candle straightens.

The droplets still.

The string goes quiet.

Rowan's face shifts— just slightly.

"Again."

The journal opens.

"Control is not suppression. Control is choice."

The droplets lift without instruction.

The flame freezes.

"I didn't—"

"I know."

Respect. Caution.

"Bring them down."

They settle.

Rowan watches me carefully.

"You're loud," she says.

"Who's listening?"

"Not everything that hears you will be friendly."

And for the first time since the spoon slid across my counter, I feel it again—

That sense that the world isn't just responding.

It's watching.

Chapter
- 9 -
The Ripple

I don't practice that night.

Not because Rowan told me not to.

Because I don't trust the quiet.

You're loud.

The words won't leave me alone.

What did she mean by that?

The house feels normal when I get home.

Shoes by the door. Backpacks half-zipped. One sock in the hallway that no one claims ownership of. The dishwasher humming like it always does.

But normal isn't the same as unaware.

I can feel it now.

The space between things.

The way the air seems to hold its breath when I enter a room.

I stand in my kitchen and stare at the counter where the spoon moved.

The sunlight is gone now. Evening has settled in soft and gray.

I don't reach.

I don't even think about reaching.

But something in me hums low anyway.

Like a wire that's been connected.

Dinner is loud.

Blessedly loud.

The girls argue about homework. One of them spills milk. Someone complains about broccoli like it's a personal attack.

It's chaotic in the ordinary way. The good kind of loud. Not the kind that feels like a warning.

And for a moment, I feel relief.

Because this kind of noise doesn't listen.

This kind of noise is just normal.

But when I stand at the sink rinsing plates, the water slows.

Not stops.

Slows.

Just enough for me to notice.

My hands freeze under the stream.

I didn't ask.

I didn't reach.

I didn't even think.

The faucet resumes its normal pressure like nothing happened.

My pulse doesn't race.

It drops.

Rowan's voice echoes in my head.

You're loud.

I whisper to myself, "What the hell does that even mean?"

Later, when the house is finally calm again, I sit on the edge of my bed with the journal in my lap.

I don't open it.

I don't need to.

The air feels … thick.

Not heavy.

Present.

The attic door creaks.

Not open.

Just a shift.

Wood settling.

Or something else.

I stare at the ceiling.

"I'm not practicing," I whisper.

Silence.

And then—

A faint tapping sound.

Not from above.

From the hallway.

I stand slowly.

The girls' doors are closed. Their breathing is soft and steady.

The hallway light flickers once.

Just once.

And steadies.

My stomach tightens.

"I'm not doing that," I say.

From the corner of my eye, the framed photo at the end of the hall tilts slightly.

Not falling.

Tilting.

Like someone brushed past it.

I step closer.

It's my grandmother.

Young. Sharp-eyed. Certain.

The glass feels cool when I straighten it.

"Is this you?" I whisper.

The air doesn't answer.

But it shifts.

That low hum inside me answers instead.

Not from anger.

Not from fear.

From awareness.

Rowan's words settle heavier now.

Power like yours doesn't whisper for long.

I stand there in the dim hallway and, for the first time, I think I understand what she meant.

It isn't just that I'm louder.

It's that something else can now hear the frequency.

Across town

A candle flickers in a room without windows.

A woman pauses mid-sentence.

Her head cocks slightly.

The others go silent without being told.

She smiles.

"Finally," she says.

Back in my hallway, the air settles.

The hum inside me goes still.

But it doesn't disappear.

It waits.

And for the first time since I moved a spoon across my counter, I realize something else moved too.

Not in my house.

In the world.

Chapter
- 10 -
Ink

I don't mean to practice.

But I absolutely do.

The house settles into that late-night mundane — dishwasher off, girls asleep, hallway light dim — and instead of avoiding it, I walk straight into my kitchen like I've got something to prove.

I set a candle in the center of the table.

I stare at it.

"You are not about to burn this house down," I tell myself. Out loud. Because apparently that's who I am now. A woman negotiating with wax.

I roll my shoulders once.

Rowan made it look easy.

She didn't even blink.

I hover my hand over the wick.

My heart is pounding way too hard for something that is technically just … fire.

"Okay," I say. "Let's not be dramatic."

I close my eyes for a second.

Inhale.

Exhale.

That warmth is there immediately.

Not wild.

Waiting.

I pull it up slowly, like drawing water from a well I didn't know I had.

Down my arm.

Into my palm.

The air tightens.

Just a little.

And then—

The wick catches.

A clean flame snaps to life under my hand.

I jerk back so fast I nearly knock the chair over.

"Oh, hell."

The flame steadies.

It doesn't leap.

It doesn't rage.

It just … exists.

Exactly where I told it to.

I stare at it.

Then I start laughing.

Not hysterically.

Not manic.

Just disbelieving.

"Are you fucking kidding me?" I whisper.

I glance around my empty kitchen like someone might witness this.

No one does.

Good.

Because I don't think I could explain this without sounding like a total nut case.

I sit down slowly.

"Well," I say, "since we're here."

I focus on the flame again.

"Higher."

It rises.

Controlled.

"Lower."

It dips.

Obedient.

My pulse is racing now, but not from fear.

From thrill.

I move my hand slowly over the flame the way Rowan did.

It doesn't burn.

It leans.

Like it recognizes me.

That thought should scare me.

Instead, it makes my chest ache.

I snuff the flame between my fingers.

A thin ribbon of smoke curls into the air.

I grin despite myself.

"I was about to give up on you," I say.

The hum inside me answers.

Not chaotic.

Not loud.

Steady.

And suddenly I need to tell her.

Grandma.

Upstairs, I sit on the edge of my bed with the journal in my lap.

I wasn't planning on opening it.

But my hands move anyway.

I flip past the familiar pages.

Past my grandmother's careful handwriting.

Past notes about herbs and containment.

And then I find a blank page.

Completely blank.

I don't know why that unsettles me.

I grab the pen from my nightstand.

It feels stupid.

Writing to a dead woman.

But I do it anyway.

I press the tip of the pen to the paper.

Dear Grandma, today I—

The ink bleeds.

Not drips.

Bleeds.

Like the paper is drinking it.

I freeze.

The words don't smear.

They don't scratch out.

They dissolve.

Slowly.

Each letter fading into the page like it was never mine to begin with.

"What the hell," I whisper.

The line disappears completely.

The page is blank again.

And then—

New ink rises.

Not from the pen.

From the paper itself.

Dark.

Certain.

Slanted the way I remember.

My grandmother's handwriting.

It forms slowly, one word at a time.

If you are reading this, then you have returned.

My body goes completely still.

Returned.

Not begun.

Not discovered.

Returned.

The next line forms.

I could not leave everything written.

Some truths must wait for strength.

The words settle into the page like they belong there.

One more line appears.

You are closer than you think.

The ink dries instantly.

Like it was always there.

I don't move.

I don't blink.

I don't breathe.

She timed this.

Not randomly.

Not accidentally.

She knew I would reach this point.

And she knew I would be alone when I did.

I close the journal slowly.

Carefully.

The hum inside me isn't loud tonight.

It's patient.

After opening that trunk in the attic, I don't feel like I'm chasing answers now.

I feel like something is waiting for me to catch up.

Chapter
- 11 -
Timing

Two days pass by before I try to read and write in the journal again.

Two days of pretending I'm fine with "returned."

Two days of that word sitting in the back of my skull, taking up way too much room, slowly building pressure in my brain.

I wait until the house is hushed again.

I don't light a candle this time.

No theatrics.

No warm-up.

I sit at the kitchen table and open the journal straight to a blank page.

"Okay," I say. "You don't get to just drop something like that on me and disappear."

I press the pen to paper.

Grandma, tell me more.

The ink bleeds instantly.

No hesitation.

No drama.

It seeps into the page like it was never mine.

I don't even flinch this time.

I wait.

Handwriting rises slowly and deliberate.

When it is time.

That's it.

No elaboration.

No comfort.

No explanation.

I stare at the words.

"That's not helpful," I say.

I flip forward.

Blank page.

I write again.

What time?

The ink stays.

Nothing bleeds.

Nothing shifts.

Just my own handwriting staring back at me like I'm the idiot in this situation.

I close the journal harder than I mean to.

"When it is time," I repeat under my breath. "That's vague as hell."

The phone rings.

I jump.

The school's number flashes across the screen.

My stomach drops.

The principal's office smells like old paper and disappointment.

Rose is sitting in the chair outside the office when I walk in.

Her arms are crossed.

Chin on her chest.

No tears.

No fear.

Just anger.

There's a faint red mark across her knuckles.

The principal clears her throat when I step inside.

"Mrs. Grace, thank you for coming."

"What happened?" I ask, keeping my voice level.

Rose doesn't look at me.

The principal folds her hands.

"There was an incident at recess."

That word.

Incident.

Like it was weather.

"A boy in her class was teasing another student," she continues. "It escalated."

Rose exhales sharply through her nose.

"He tried to grab her," she says.

The principal's lips tighten.

"He attempted to touch her inappropriately."

"Inappropriately how?" I ask, already knowing.

Rose answers before the principal can.

"He tried to grab her butt."

Silence fills the room.

"And you punched him," I say, still calm.

Rose finally looks at me.

"I told him to stop."

Her voice is steady.

"He laughed."

Her jaw tightens.

"So, I punched him."

"How hard?" I ask.

Rose shrugs.

"Hard enough."

The principal clears her throat again.

"The other student required ice and a brief visit to the nurse. There was bleeding."

"From?" I ask steadily.

"His lip," she replies.

Her expression suggests that it isn't the point.

I turn to Rose.

"Did he touch you?"

"No."

"But he touched her?"

"He tried."

"And you didn't think to get a teacher?"

Rose's eyes flash.

"He thought he could just do what he wanted."

That's the only explanation she offers.

Like that alone justified it.

On the drive home, the car is quiet for about thirty seconds.

Then Rose exhales dramatically.

"That asshole deserved it."

"Language!" I shout immediately.

She rolls her eyes.

"He is an asshole."

"Rose."

She slumps back in her seat.

"Fine. He's a jerk."

I grip the steering wheel a little tighter.

"You don't get to hit people because you're angry."

"I wasn't angry."

Her tone sharpens.

"I was stopping him."

"That's not how that works."

She turns toward me now.

"You always said if we get in a fight, don't lose."

I sigh.

"That was not permission to start one."

"I didn't start it."

Her voice rises.

"I finished it."

I glance at her.

Her eyes are bright.

Not guilty.

Not ashamed.

Certain.

"I punched that asshole straight in the mouth," she says. "Shut him up real quick."

"Rose."

"What? It worked."

I pull into the driveway and put the car in park.

The engine ticks as it cools.

I turn to face her fully.

"You don't let anger decide how you protect someone."

"I wasn't angry."

"You were."

Her mouth opens to argue.

I hold up a hand.

"You can protect your friends. You can stand up for yourself. But you don't get to lose control while you do it."

She frowns.

"I didn't lose."

"That's not what I mean."

She looks away, jaw set.

"Then what do you mean?"

I study her for a second.

Twelve-years-old.

All fire and certainty.

"No matter how right you are," I say quietly, "there's always a way to do it without becoming the thing you're fighting."

She doesn't respond to that.

She just stares out the window.

Inside, I feel that familiar hum.

Not magic.

Just something heavy.

Timing.

Control.

Force.

Reaction.

I think about the journal.

When it is time.

Rose opens the door and climbs out.

"I'd do it again," she says, before slamming it shut.

I sit there for a moment longer.

Then I reach into my bag and pull out the journal.

I don't open it.

I just rest my hand on the cover.

"When it is time," I repeat quietly.

I wonder if "when it is time" wasn't only about magic.

Chapter
- 12 -
The Work

I don't wait long before going back to Rowan's house.

Two days.

That's all the patience I can manage.

The journal sits heavy in my bag the entire drive there.

When it is time.

I hate that answer. It kind of pisses me off that Grandma left me hanging like that.

Rowan opens the door before I knock.

She studies my face like she's measuring something.

"You look irritated," she says.

"I am."

She steps aside.

"Good."

That's not the response I expected.

Inside, her house feels the same — herbs drying, cats watching, everything in its place. The air is steady here. Intentional.

I set the journal on her kitchen table.

"It answered me again."

Rowan's eyebrow lifts slightly.

"What did you ask?"

"Grandma, tell me more."

"And?"

"When it is time, arose from the page."

Rowan goes still.

Not dramatic.

Not surprised.

Just… alert.

"You wrote her to tell you more?"

"Yes."

"And the ink bled?"

"Yes."

"What do you feel about the answer?"

I hesitate.

"Shut down. Like she slammed a door in my face."

Rowan nods slowly.

"That's not common."

I narrow my eyes.

"That's not reassuring."

Rowan meets my gaze evenly.

"It means the binding is stronger than I thought."

"Stronger how?"

She rests her hand on the cover but doesn't open it.

"Bloodline magic can be responsive. But yours is… selective."

I don't know if that's a compliment.

"Selective how?"

"It reveals by readiness, not request."

I cross my arms.

"I'm ready."

Rowan's mouth almost curves.

"No," she says calmly. "You're impatient."

That lands.

She steps away from the table.

"We're done with flame work."

Good.

I don't say that out loud, but she sees it in my face.

"We move to precision."

She walks to a drawer and pulls out a spoon.

Metal.

Plain.

Unremarkable.

She places it on the counter between us.

"Seven days," she says. "You bend it a little more each night."

"How much?"

"Enough to feel it. Not enough to lose control."

I stare at the spoon.

"And if I bend it in half tonight?"

"You won't."

That confidence irritates me.

"Why?"

"Because control is not force."

She steps back.

"Do it."

I inhale slowly.

Exhale slower.

I don't reach outward.

I reach inward.

The warmth answers immediately now.

Not wild.

Present.

I look at the spoon.

I don't picture it snapping.

I picture it softening.

The metal trembles.

Just slightly.

Then dips.

Barely.

A shallow curve forms in the neck of it.

I stop.

Rowan nods once.

"Again tomorrow."

That's it.

No applause.

No awe.

Just expectation.

She moves to the center of the kitchen and places two wooden chairs on opposite sides of the room.

"Assignment two."

She gestures.

"Bring them closer together."

"How close?"

"Not touching."

I focus.

This is heavier.

The air thickens almost immediately.

The chairs scrape—slow, controlled—across the floor.

An inch.

Two.

Three.

I stop before my pulse rises.

Rowan watches my breathing.

"Good," she says.

"Put them back."

I do, exactly where they were.

Precision.

Control.

Reset.

We repeat it three times.

Each time smoother.

Each time quieter.

On the fourth attempt, something shifts.

A flicker.

Like static at the edge of my awareness.

I pause.

Rowan notices.

"What?"

"Nothing," I say quickly.

But it wasn't nothing.

It felt like … pressure.

Like someone leaning toward a door on the other side.

It fades as soon as I stop.

Rowan studies me.

"You felt it."

I don't ask how she knows.

"Yes."

"Describe it."

"Like … something listening. It's hard to explain."

Rowan's jaw tightens.

"That will stop."

"When?"

"When you learn to dim."

"You haven't told me how to do that."

She steps closer.

"Because you don't know what you are yet."

That doesn't feel comforting.

She circles me once like she's measuring posture.

"Dimming is not hiding. It's compression."

"Compression?"

"Think of it like lowering a flame without extinguishing it."

"I thought we were done with flames."

"We are."

She holds my gaze.

"But the metaphor still stands."

I close my eyes.

I imagine the warmth inside me folding inward.

Not disappearing.

Condensing.

Like pulling fabric tight around something bright.

The room shifts.

Subtle.

But real.

The air lightens.

Rowan nods slowly.

"Again."

I do it.

Faster this time.

Cleaner.

By the third attempt, the static feeling doesn't return.

Rowan watches me carefully.

"You won't feel watched when you do it correctly."

"And if I don't?"

"You will."

She doesn't elaborate.

Of course, she doesn't.

She returns to the spoon and sets it back on the counter.

"Seven days," she repeats, tapping the spoon lightly against the table. "A little more each time. No rushing."

"And the chairs?"

"Closer each night."

"And dimming?"

"Every session. Before and after."

I exhale.

This isn't flashy.

It isn't dramatic.

It's work.

Good.

I can do work.

As I gather my things, Rowan rests her hand briefly on the journal.

"Do not force it," she says quietly.

"I wasn't."

"You were going to."

She's right.

I wanted to rush home and bend the spoon completely in half just to see if I could.

On the drive home, the spoon rests in my bag beside the journal.

It feels heavier than it should.

Not because it's metal.

Because now it's a promise.

Seven days.

I don't practice that night.

Not because I'm afraid.

Because I'm disciplined.

That feels new.

And steady.

And maybe—

Just maybe—

Like progress.

Chapter
- 13 -
Ladies Night

The piano lounge smells like polished wood and expensive perfume.

Low amber light pools across velvet chairs and small round tables. Candles flicker in shallow glass bowls. The piano in the corner hums through something jazzy and slow, the kind of music that makes you sit up a little straighter without meaning to.

Maddie is already halfway through her martini when I slide into the booth.

Her pink hair is twisted up tonight, like she's trying to look refined and failing beautifully.

"Finally," she says. "I was about to order you something irresponsible."

"I drove," I say.

She waves a hand. "Details."

Across from us, JoAnne is mid-rant about her ex-husband's new girlfriend, who apparently "has the personality of a damp sponge."

Emma laughs too loudly. Taylor nods like she's taking mental notes for a future intervention. Lucy swirls her wine with unnecessary aggression.

Normal.

Loud in the best way.

Rowan sits at the edge of the couch, one leg crossed over the other, a glass of red wine untouched in her hand. She looks like she belongs in a painting.

Her eyes flick to mine.

A quiet check-in.

I nod once.

Dimmed.

Controlled.

I remember.

Maddie leans in close. "Okay, but seriously, what is different about you?"

I blink. "Nothing."

"Bullshit," JoAnne says. "You look … glowy."

Lucy squints at me. "Did you get Botox?"

"God, I wish," I say.

Taylor tilts her head. "Are you dating someone? Did you get laid?"

I choke on my first sip of wine.

"No."

Maddie grins. "She's absolutely seeing someone."

"I am not."

"You definitely look like someone who got laid," says JoAnne, confidently.

The table erupts.

I roll my eyes. "Y'all are drunk."

"Not yet," says Maddie, twirling her finger in the air to signal the server for another round.

The piano shifts keys, smooth and warm.

The conversation drifts the way it always does — kids, work, aging parents, someone's failed diet attempt.

Then Maddie says it.

"Men are trash."

JoAnne raises her glass. "To cheating exes."

The laughter shifts.

It sharpens.

I feel it before I react to it.

That old tightness in my chest.

Two marriages.

Two betrayals.

The humiliation of pretending I didn't see it coming.

Maddie's eyes flick to me.

Rowan's wine glass stills midair.

"Some of them are," I say, evenly.

JoAnne snorts. "All of them."

I reach for my glass.

Just wine.

Just a sip.

Just normal.

The warmth inside me flares before I can stop it.

Not rage.

Memory.

And the candle on our table leans.

Just slightly.

The piano hits a chord—

—and it sustains too long.

A single note stretching thin across the room.

Every wine glass at our table vibrates.

Not violently.

Just enough.

The red wine ripples.

The white shivers.

Ice cracks in someone's cocktail with a sharp little pop.

Silence falls around our booth for half a breath.

Then—

JoAnne bursts out laughing. "Okay, damn, Izzy. We get it."

Lucy claps once. "That struck a nerve."

Emma squints at the candle. "Did that just—?"

"Static," I say quickly, forcing a shrug. "I swear I attract it. It's a whole thing."

"Who gets shocked by a wine glass?" JoAnne says.

"Me," I reply. "Apparently."

They're already moving on.

Back to jokes.

Back to wine.

Back to normal.

Maddie doesn't laugh.

Rowan doesn't blink.

The piano player shakes his head slightly, like he hit the wrong pedal.

The room resumes.

Conversation swells.

But Rowan leans in close enough that only I can hear her.

"You didn't dim."

My stomach drops.

"I did."

"No."

Her voice is calm.

Certain.

"You felt it spike."

I stare down into my wine.

"Yeah."

"And?"

I swallow.

"I forgot."

Rowan studies my face.

"You're not allowed to forget."

Shame prickles hotter than the magic did.

"I know."

Maddie squeezes my knee under the table.

Not judgment.

Just acknowledgment.

We stay another hour.

I laugh.

I drink.

I let the noise wash over me.

But I dim.

Carefully.

Intentionally.

When we step outside into the cooler night air, I pause on the sidewalk.

The city feels ordinary again.

Traffic.

Voices.

I compress the warmth inside me.

Fold it inward.

Quiet.

Controlled.

Rowan watches, satisfied.

Maddie loops her arm through mine.

"You're getting stronger," she whispers.

I glance back at the lounge doors.

The candles inside flicker once, then settle.

"Yeah," I say, softly.

"I know."

Chapter
- 14 -
The Listening

ay five.

The spoon is almost bent in half.

Not snapped. Not twisted violently.

But curved deep enough that it no longer looks accidental.

Two days left.

I stand barefoot in my kitchen, sunlight stretching across the counter where this all started.

The chairs move without scraping now. They glide toward each other smoothly, stopping inches apart in the center of the room.

I lift my hand slightly.

They slide back.

Exactly where they began.

Precision.

Control.

Reset.

Before.

After.

I dim.

The compression comes easier now. Like flexing a muscle instead of discovering one.

The static feeling hasn't returned in two days.

That should comfort me.

It doesn't.

It feels like something stepped back.

Watching from farther away.

Waiting.

I pick up the spoon and run my thumb along the bend.

Five days of discipline.

Five days of resisting the urge to just snap it in half to prove I can.

I could.

I know I could.

That's not the point.

I set it down gently and reach for the journal.

No candle.

No theatrics.

Just afternoon light and the quiet hum of my house while the girls are at school.

I flip to a blank page.

Grandma, I feel watched, I write.

The ink bleeds.

Slower than before.

Like it's weighing, thinking, studying whether I'm ready.

My handwriting dissolves.

Hers rises.

You are being sensed.

The Below stirs when our blood rises.

You were hidden once for protection.

You will not be hidden again.

Control yourself before they force you to.

You are stronger than you know.

I stare at the words.

Hidden once.

Force me to what?

My pulse slows instead of spikes.

That feels intentional.

I close the journal carefully.

Not panicked.

Focused.

I grab my keys.

Rowan opens the door before I knock.

Her eyes go straight to my face.

"What did it say?" she asks.

I don't step inside yet.

"What is the Below?"

Her expression doesn't change.

She steps aside.

"Come in."

Her house feels grounded. Steady.

The cats are alert but still. The herbs don't sway.

I place the journal on her kitchen table.

"It said I'm being sensed," I tell her. "That the Below stirs when our blood rises. That I was hidden once. That I won't be hidden again."

Rowan's jaw tightens slightly.

Not surprised.

Resolved.

"If there's a Below," I ask, meeting her eyes, "what's Above?"

"Us," she says, immediately.

"Us?" I repeat.

"The Above," Rowan clarifies. "We live on the surface. We blend. We control. We conceal. We do not draw from what corrupts."

"And the Below?" I press.

"They draw from something older. Heavier." Rowan moves toward the window as she speaks, voice level. "It gives power quickly. It takes more than it gives."

"Like demons?" I ask. "Are we talking Harry Potter magic or some Rosemary's Baby demon shit?"

Rowan turns back to face me.

"Neither."

Her tone is firm.

"This isn't fantasy. And it isn't possession. It's inheritance."

Inheritance.

That word hits heavier than anything else she's said.

"Then what is it?" I demand. "Because I feel like I'm walking around with a target on my back and nobody wants to tell me why."

"You feel watched because you are visible," Rowan says calmly.

"I've been dimming."

"Yes. And you're improving."

"That's not comforting."

"It shouldn't be."

She folds her hands loosely in front of her.

"When your bloodline went quiet, they assumed it ended."

My stomach tightens.

"When it rose again," she continues, "it sent a ripple."

"Ladies Night," I say.

Rowan nods once.

"You didn't just disturb glass. You disturbed air."

I swallow.

"So who exactly is 'they'?"

"The Below is not monsters," Rowan replies quietly. "It's people."

That's worse.

"People who believe power should be taken, not refined. People who resent restraint. People who would have preferred your bloodline stay buried."

Buried.

"You said I was hidden once."

Rowan holds my gaze.

"You were."

"From what?"

"After your mother died, your grandmother removed you from certain territories."

"Territories?" I repeat.

"Below-controlled spaces."

"I grew up here."

"Yes."

"That's not what I'm asking."

There's a pause.

"You were present when lines were crossed," says Rowan, carefully.

"I was a child."

"Yes."

"And your grandmother decided you would not be raised where blood politics rule."

Blood politics.

The phrase makes my chest tighten.

"I have two daughters," I say, quietly. "If something is stirring, I need to know what I'm dealing with."

"This is not about demons," says Rowan, firmly. "No one is coming for your children."

"Yet?"

"No."

Her answer is immediate.

Certain.

"The Below does not target children," she adds. "They target power."

"And that's me."

"Yes."

Silence stretches between us.

"Am I in danger?" I ask.

Rowan studies me before answering.

"You are visible."

I exhale slowly.

"If they draw from corruption," I ask, "what do we draw from?"

"Balance."

"That sounds nice. It doesn't sound powerful."

"It's slower," Rowan says. "But it lasts."

I think about the spoon nearly bending in half.

The chairs gliding.

The dimming coming easier.

"You think they'll come?" I ask.

"They already noticed."

The words settle in my bones.

"Then, what's next?"

Rowan's voice shifts slightly. Less explanation. More directive.

"You stop training like it's a hobby."

Her eyes sharpen.

"You train like survival."

Something in me understands that she isn't being dramatic.

She's being honest

I nod once.

"Then we speed it up?"

"Yes."

I finally don't feel confused for the first time since all this shit started.

I feel aligned.

Above.

Below.

Hidden once.

Visible now.

Inheritance.

As I step outside into the late afternoon light, I dim instinctively.

Compression.

Control.

Across town, beneath older streets where tradition is strictly followed—

a woman pauses mid-sentence.

The others at the table fall silent without being told.

She closes her eyes.

Feels it.

Not new.

But louder.

She opens her eyes.

"She's awake," she says.

No one asks who.

They already know.

Chapter
- 15 -
Breaking Point

I don't sleep.

Not really.

I lie there in the dark with my eyes open, listening to the house breathe and trying to pretend the quiet doesn't feel different now.

Like it's leaning closer.

Like it's listening back.

By morning, I've had enough.

The girls are at school. The dishwasher is running. The world is doing its normal little routines like nothing in my life has shifted.

I sit at the kitchen table with the journal in front of me, hands flat on either side of it like I'm about to negotiate.

I don't light a candle.

No warm-up.

No theatrics.

I open straight to a blank page.

"Okay," I say. "If you're going to start dropping real words now, then we're going to have a real conversation."

My pen hovers for half a second.

Then I press it down.

Grandma. Who is listening?

The ink bleeds.

Immediately.

No hesitation.

It spreads into the page like it's eager. Like it's been waiting for that exact question.

My handwriting fades like it never existed.

Hers rises in its place.

Marlene.

That's the first word.

Just sitting there by itself like a name can be a weapon. Like I'm just supposed to know who the fuck Marlene is.

My throat tightens.

The ink keeps moving.

Marlene ended your mother.

The pen slips slightly in my fingers. Not because I'm shaking—yet but because my brain refuses to catch up with what my eyes are reading.

Ended.

Not lost.

Not died.

Not accident.

Ended.

I stare at the line until it blurs.

"No," I whisper, like the page might take it back if I say it out loud.

The ink continues anyway.

Your father was not the target.

I blink hard.

My chest feels tight and hollow at the same time, like someone punched straight through me and left a giant hole.

I swallow.

A sound escapes my mouth that's half laugh, half choke.

"Are you fucking kidding me?" I whisper.

My hands go cold.

Then my fingertips start to burn.

Not metaphorically.

Physically.

Heat flares up through my palms like my blood just remembered something it's been trying to forget for decades.

The kitchen around me sharpens.

Every sound gets too loud.

The hum of the fridge.

The drip of the faucet.

The faint tick of the clock on the wall.

Marlene ended your mother.

I read it again.

And again.

And then something in me snaps— not like breaking glass or exploding cabinets.

Like a door that's been held shut for years finally opening.

A low sound builds in my ears, like pressure.

Like a storm trying to climb out through my skin.

I push the journal away from me too hard. It slides across the table and goes over the edge, landing on the floor like it weighs a hundred pounds.

My breath comes out sharp.

No.

No, no, no!

My parents died in a car accident.

That's what I've been told my whole life.

That's what the world decided was true.

That's what my grandmother let me believe.

And now a page is telling me it wasn't a tragedy.

It was a choice.

A person made it.

A woman with a name made it.

Marlene.

My fingers curl around the spoon on the counter before I even realize I've reached for it.

Day six.

This was supposed to be careful. Controlled. A little more bend, then stop.

Two days left.

I stare at the spoon in my hand.

The metal looks innocent.

Normal.

Like it doesn't know it's about to witness something ugly.

The candle sits on the table near the journal. I didn't light it earlier.

I don't have to.

I lift my hand over the wick, the way Rowan did, without thinking.

The flame catches instantly.

Too instantly.

It flares high, bright and hungry, like it was waiting— a flame burning too hot.

My whole body feels like heat now.

Not anger exactly.

Something deeper.

Grief with teeth.

Betrayal.

The humiliation of realizing you've been living inside a lie.

My fingers burn.

The spoon starts to tremble.

I inhale.

I try to dim.

It doesn't take.

The warmth doesn't fold. It surges.

"Are you fucking kidding me?" I say again, louder this time, like the words might cut through the pressure building inside my chest.

The spoon bends.

Not slowly.

Not gently.

It curls like the metal has turned soft as wax.

It goes past half.

Past what Rowan told me to do.

Past restraint.

The two ends curl inward, tightening, folding until the spoon is no longer a spoon at all.

It becomes a clenched fist of metal.

A knot.

A ball.

And I don't stop it.

I feel it.

I let it. It relieves the pressure building inside me.

Somewhere in the living room, wood groans.

I don't even look up before it happens.

The two wooden chairs—placed on opposite sides of the room like Rowan instructed—slam together like something invisible grabbed them and decided it was done being gentle.

The impact is violent.

Final.

Wood splinters.

A crack like a gunshot.

Then another.

Then the sound of pieces scattering across the floor.

Silence follows so fast it feels like the house is holding its breath again.

I stand there with the ruined spoon in my hand, candle flame towering on the table, my chest rising and falling too hard.

The air is thick.

Not haunted.

Not mysterious.

Charged.

And for one second, I feel it— something at the edge of my awareness.

Not inside my house.

Outside it.

Like a head turning.

Like attention.

I freeze.

My heartbeat pounds once.

Twice.

Then I force myself to dim.

I close my eyes, drop to my knees and compress, fold inward, and clamp down like my life depends on it.

The warmth resists; angry in its own right.

I breathe through it.

Again.

Again.

Finally, it sinks.

Not gone.

Contained.

The candle flame lowers until it's normal again.

My fingertips stop burning.

The air loosens by degrees.

I look toward the living room.

The chairs are gone.

Not moved.

Destroyed.

There is nothing left but jagged wood and broken legs and splinters scattered like evidence.

My stomach drops.

I whisper, softer now, "Shit."

And I don't know if I'm saying it because I'm scared of what I just did…

Or because a part of me feels like it finally got to scream.

The girls come home that afternoon, not knowing anything happened.

Backpacks hit the floor.

Shoes are kicked off.

A question is shouted down the hall about snacks.

Normal noise. Normal mess. Normal life.

Rose is the first to notice.

She stops in the living room doorway, eyes scanning the space like she's doing inventory.

"Where are the chairs?" she asks.

I don't miss a beat.

I'm at the sink, rinsing a cup like I'm not standing on top of splinters and lies.

"They didn't match the decor," I say evenly. "I donated them."

Rose squints at me. "You loved those chairs."

"I changed my mind."

She makes a face like she doesn't believe me.

Because she doesn't.

From the hallway, Lily's voice floats in. "Mom? Did you seriously donate the chairs?"

"Yes," I call back, too quick.

There's a pause.

Then Lily, quieter, mostly to herself: "That's weird."

I grip the edge of the counter a little tighter.

Rose shrugs eventually, already moving on. "Whatever. Can I have chips?"

"After dinner," I say, quickly.

The day continues.

Homework. Complaints. A slammed door. A laugh.

And I do not look at the living room floor again.

Not until they're asleep.

I stand in the kitchen with the ruined spoon in my hand, the journal closed on the table.

My pulse is steady now.

Too steady.

Like the storm burned itself out and left ash behind.

I run my thumb along the warped metal.

I can't even pretend this was an accident.

I made that choice.

I let it happen.

Because the truth made me want to break something.

And I did.

The front porch creaks.

Not the attic.

Not settling wood.

A deliberate sound.

My head snaps up.

The knock comes once, then the door opens without waiting.

Rowan steps inside like she owns the place.

She doesn't look surprised.

She looks tired.

Her eyes sweep the kitchen, then flick toward the living room, like she can see what happened without needing proof.

Her gaze lands on my hand.

On the ruined spoon.

"You let it burn," she says, quietly.

Not angry.

Not loud.

Mature.

Disappointed in the way that hurts me more than if she yelled.

My throat tightens.

"I found out," I say.

Rowan's eyes sharpen. "What did the journal say?"

I swallow, then force the words out.

"It said a woman named Marlene ended my mother."

Rowan doesn't flinch.

That alone makes my stomach turn.

"You knew," I whisper.

Rowan steps closer, stopping just short of the table. "I suspected. Your grandmother confirmed enough over the years."

My hands are shaking now. Just slightly.

"Everyone told me it was a car accident," I say, voice rising. "My whole damn life."

Rowan's expression doesn't soften. She keeps it steady— like she's bracing the room.

"That's what they wanted you to believe."

"They?" I snap. "The Below, the Above, who— everyone?"

Rowan's jaw tightens.

"Yes."

I laugh once, sharp and ugly. "She murdered my mother and they called weather."

Rowan's eyes flick toward the journal.

"Marlene doesn't call herself that anymore," she says.

I stare at her. "What?"

Rowan's voice is flat. Controlled. "She goes by Mara now."

Mara.

The name feels different.

Shorter.

Sharper.

Like it was chosen.

Like she cut off the soft parts of herself and kept what was useful.

I feel heat rise again, quick and dangerous.

Rowan sees it.

"Dim," she says immediately.

"I am dimmed."

"No," replies Rowan, stepping closer. "You're clenching."

I hate how she's right.

I hate how she can see me.

I force the compression again, so I slow my breathing, lock my jaw.

Rowan watches until the air loosens.

Then she speaks, lower.

"You can be angry," she says. "But you cannot be careless."

I gesture toward the living room with the ruined spoon in my hand. "I didn't burn the house down," I say, choking back tears.

"That is not the standard," says Rowan, sharply. "That is the bare minimum."

Those words hurt.

Good.

I needed them.

I swallow, fighting the sting in my eyes.

"Why didn't Grandma tell me?" I ask, and my voice cracks around the question like it's been waiting years to be asked.

Rowan's gaze softens just a fraction.

"Because names have consequences," she says. "And because she was trying to give you a childhood before the war remembered you."

War.

That word makes the kitchen feel colder.

Rowan looks at the ruined spoon again.

Then at me.

"She felt that," Rowan says.

I go still.

"Mara," Rowan clarifies. "She felt that surge."

My stomach tightens.

"And she smiled," adds Rowan, quietly, like she hates saying it. "Because she can feel you're angry."

I stare at Rowan, the truth settling into my bones like a weight.

"So, what now?" I ask.

Rowan's eyes hold mine.

Now she isn't teacher.

She isn't guide.

She's something closer to an ally.

"Now," she says, "we stop pretending this is just training."

I nod once, slowly.

The candle flame flickers.

Then steadies.

In the quiet, the journal sits closed on the table like a mouth that has finally started telling the truth.

And outside my house, the night feels wider than it used to.

Not empty.

Occupied.

Listening.

Waiting.

And somewhere, in a place I've never seen but suddenly believe in with my whole body— a woman named Mara is smiling into the dark.

Chapter
- 16 -
Stalked

I don't sleep much.

Not because I'm scared of the dark.

Because my brain won't stop replaying today like a TikTok reel.

The words. The heat. The sound of wood cracking like a gunshot in my living room.

Marlene.

Mara.

I lie there staring at the ceiling, listening to the house breathe, trying to pretend I'm still the kind of woman who believes things happen for a fucking reason.

By morning, the quiet feels like a dare.

The girls leave for school with the usual noise— zippers, shoes, a shouted goodbye that turns into an argument halfway down the hall. Lily calls something "literally insane." Rose slams the door like it personally offended her.

Normal.

I hold onto that like a railing.

The second the bus pulls away, I go into the living room and just stand there.

The broken chairs are gone, but small jagged pieces and splinters remain, scattered like the house had shed skin. I cleaned up enough that the girls didn't notice I had made the chairs duel one another.

I stare at the emptiness and feel something in my chest try to flare again—shame, anger, grief, all tangled up and sharp.

I don't let it.

I breathe.

Slow.

Then slower.

I dim.

Compression. Folding inward. Clamping down— not to hide, but to contain.

The air lightens, just a fraction.

I grab a trash bag and start sweeping up the tiny pieces that remain.

It's not dramatic.

It's not cinematic.

It's me in leggings and an old T-shirt, sweeping up evidence like I'm cleaning up after I committed a crime.

I bag the splinters; the sad little screws I missed that once held everything together.

I don't look at the spot where the chairs used to sit.

I refuse to give that moment much reverence.

When the floor is finally clear, I mop twice.

Like soap and water can erase a lie.

Then, I open my laptop and order new chairs.

Not replacements.

Not the same.

Different.

Heavier. Modern. Clean lines. Something that looks like a decision instead of a memory.

I click the purchase button with more satisfaction than I should.

There.

Something changed, and I changed something back.

That's control.

I tell myself that.

I need to believe it.

Later, I stand in the kitchen with the spoon in my hand.

A new spoon.

Because the old one is a knotted ball of metal sitting in the trash like an accusation.

Day six.

I should bend it a little more and stop.

That's the assignment.

That's the work.

I dim first.

Before.

Always before.

I inhale. Exhale. Fold the warmth inward.

Then I focus on the spoon.

Not snapping.

Not curling.

Softening.

Just enough.

The metal trembles.

It dips.

A clean, controlled curve.

And I stop.

I set it down like it matters.

Because it does.

Then I move a kitchen chair and a heavy stool.

I slide them toward each other.

Slow. Quiet. Intentional.

I stop with them inches apart.

Then I reset.

Exactly where they started.

Again.

Again.

Again.

This time, the air doesn't spike.

No static feeling.

No pressure at the edge of my awareness.

That should make me feel better.

It doesn't.

It feels like something stepped back on purpose.

Like it's not gone.

It's just waiting from farther away.

I wipe my hands on a towel and glance toward the journal on the table.

Closed.

Silent.

Like it already said enough.

Marlene ended your mother.

Your father was not the target.

I don't open it again.

Not today.

I've learned my limit.

That feels new, too.

By late afternoon, I'm out of groceries and low on patience.

I grab my keys and drive to the store.

The parking lot is full of minivans and shopping carts and people who still live in a world where death comes from accidents and magic comes from movies.

Inside, the air-conditioning hits my skin like a slap.

Fluorescent lights hum overhead.

Everything is too bright, too sharp, and too normal.

I grab a cart and start walking.

Milk. Eggs. Bread. Something green that won't make my kids act like I'm poisoning them.

I'm halfway through produce when the hum inside me shifts.

Not warmth.

Not anger.

Awareness.

It's subtle. A tightening at the base of my throat. A faint pressure behind my ribs.

Like the air is paying attention again.

My hand pauses over a bag of apples.

I dim.

Compression. Fold inward. Quiet.

The pressure eases slightly.

And then something in the aisle across from me shifts, too.

Not a sound.

Not a movement I can point to.

Just … the air.

Like the atmosphere itself tightened in answer.

My fingers go cold around the apples.

I lift my head slowly.

Across the aisle, near the endcap of cereal boxes, a woman stands still.

No cart.

No basket.

Just standing there like she's waiting for someone to walk into her line of sight.

She looks normal at first glance.

Jeans. Dark sweater. Hair pulled back.

But something is off.

Not costume-off.

Not dramatic.

Wrong-off.

Like she's wearing the wrong season on her skin.

Like the light doesn't sit on her the way it should.

She's too still.

Not calm-shopper still.

Predator still.

My stomach drops.

She turns her head slightly.

Her eyes land on me.

Not curious.

Not confused.

Intent.

Measured.

Like she's evaluating a piece of meat.

My pulse jumps— then drops hard.

Cold floods my chest.

Inside me, the hum tightens.

A warning.

She doesn't smile.

She doesn't threaten.

She just keeps looking.

Long enough that my skin starts prickling.

Long enough that I know I'm not imagining it.

I glance down at my cart.

Two things in it. Apples and a box of pasta.

That's it.

My body says: leave.

I grip the cart handle and turn fast, pushing it toward the front of the store like I suddenly remembered something urgent.

I don't look back.

I breathe slowly.

I dim harder.

Compression until it feels like my ribs are wrapping around the warmth inside me.

Self-checkout.

Apples. Pasta.

I don't get the milk.

I don't get the eggs.

I leave everything except getting out.

When I glance up, she's still there.

Not closer.

Not farther.

Still watching.

Like she knew I'd run.

I pay. I grab the bag. I walk out.

I don't run until I'm through the doors.

Then, I move fast across the parking lot, keys already in my hand.

I get in the car and lock the doors immediately.

My hands are steady.

My heart is not.

Through the glass doors of the store, I see her.

Still.

Watching from inside like she doesn't care if I see her.

I start the engine of my car and pull out.

Halfway down the lot, I force myself to glance back.

She's gone.

That should make me feel better.

It doesn't.

It makes the world feel bigger.

And darker.

And closer.

By the time I pull into my driveway, my jaw hurts from clenching.

The house looks the same.

Sunlight on the porch.

A package by the door.

The neighbor's dog barking like my personal security system.

Normal.

I carry my two grocery items inside and set them on the counter.

Apples.

Pasta.

The saddest dinner plan in history.

I let out a shaky laugh that dies before it becomes real.

"Well," I say out loud to no one, "pizza night it is."

I don't open the journal.

I don't call Rowan.

Not yet.

I stand there with my hands flat on the counter, breathing through the leftover adrenaline.

Because if I speak about what happened, it becomes real in a way I can't take back.

And I already know it's real.

I felt it.

That compression across the aisle.

That answer.

Someone else out there knows how to dim.

Someone else out there felt me.

And they didn't look surprised.

They looked like they'd been waiting.

I close my eyes and compress again— quiet, controlled, deliberate.

Then I open them.

And I look around my kitchen like it might not be safe anymore.

Not because something is here.

Because something now knows I am.

And for the first time since the spoon moved in sunlight, I understand Rowan's warning in my bones.

Not everything that hears you will be friendly.

And apparently— not everything stays Below.

Chapter - 17 - Watchers

The bus pulls away in a cloud of diesel and noise.

I don't even wait until it turns the corner.

I text two words.

Coffee. Now.

Rowan replies first.

On my way.

Maddie follows seconds later.

Oh, hell yes. I need caffeine and drama.

We meet at the same coffee shop as before.

Same soft jazz overhead.

Same chalkboard menu.

Same barista who pretends not to eavesdrop.

Normal.

That word feels fragile lately.

Rowan is already seated when I walk in. Black sweater. Composed. Watching the door like she expected me.

Maddie bursts in right behind me— pink hair down today, oversized sunglasses pushed up on her head.

We grab our coffees and settle in.

She looks at my face and stops smiling.

"Okay," she says. "What happened?"

I don't ease into it.

"The journal wrote back again."

Rowan's fingers tighten slightly around her mug.

Maddie leans forward.

"What did it say?"

I swallow.

"It named her."

Silence.

Rowan doesn't blink.

Maddie's eyebrows lift.

"Marlene," I say. "It said Marlene ended my mother."

Maddie exhales slowly. "Jesus."

"She calls herself Mara now," I add, watching Rowan.

Rowan gives one small confirming nod.

Maddie sits back. "Okay. That tracks."

I stare at her. "That tracks?"

Maddie shrugs. "People who reinvent themselves usually shorten their names. Makes them feel sharper."

Rowan doesn't smile.

I press on.

"I went to the grocery store yesterday. I felt something shift. Like someone answered when I dimmed."

Rowan's eyes sharpen.

"There was a woman," I say. "No cart. No basket. Just standing there watching me. She scared the fuck out of me. I grabbed two things and got the hell out of dodge."

Maddie lets out a low whistle.

"Was she from Below?" I ask.

Rowan doesn't hesitate.

"Yes."

The word lands clean and heavy.

Maddie doesn't look shocked.

She looks annoyed.

"Watcher," she says.

I blink. "Watcher?"

Rowan nods once. "Mara doesn't move without sending eyes first."

My stomach tightens.

"So, she was stalking me."

"She was confirming," Rowan corrects calmly. "You are no longer hidden."

I sit back in my chair.

"And the storefront," I say. "The one with the paper-covered windows. I parked in front of it. I saw movement behind the glass. A broom. Dishes."

Maddie's head tilts. "You found the threshold."

"You knew about it?" I snap.

Maddie snorts softly. "We all know about it."

Rowan's gaze doesn't leave mine.

"It isn't hidden," she says. "It's ignored."

The line from the journal echoes in my head.

Paper cannot hide what blood will recognize.

"Grandma wrote that," I say, quietly.

Maddie goes still for the first time since she walked in.

"She bound that journal to you?" she asks.

"Yes."

Maddie shakes her head slowly. "Your grannie was very powerful. That kind of binding? That's deep magic. Blood-sealed. It's not something you just … do."

There's a hint of admiration in her voice.

For a second, that steadies me.

Then I look at Rowan.

"Take me there."

Rowan's face looks resigned.

"I will," she says.

My pulse jumps.

"But there are rules."

I nod immediately. "Fine."

"Between now and when we go, you practice dimming. Hard."

"I have been."

"Harder," she says evenly. "You will not cross that threshold angry. You will not cross it in an emotional state."

Maddie points a finger at me. "And you definitely don't cross it trying to prove something."

Rowan continues.

"You never go alone. Ever."

I open my mouth to argue.

She cuts me off with a look.

"Ever."

I close my mouth.

"Fine."

Rowan studies me for a long moment.

"The woman in the store was not an attack," she says, quietly. "It was assessment."

"That's not comforting. I have a stalker— or whatever the fuck you want to call her."

My thoughts are a mess, but my instincts are clear.

"It shouldn't be," says Rowan, flatly.

Maddie squeezes my hand.

"Let me know when y'all are going," she says. "I'll check my schedule."

There's something in her tone I can't quite read.

Support.

Maybe calculation.

I nod anyway.

Rowan finishes her coffee and sets the cup down carefully.

"We go when you can dim without thinking about it," she says.

"How long?"

"That depends on you."

The air between us feels different now.

Not mystical.

Decided.

I came in scared.

I leave with conditions.

Practice.

Control.

No anger.

No solo heroics.

And when we go Below— I won't be walking in blind.

I'm going in with eyes wide open.

Chapter
- 18 -
Below

owan doesn't text.

She shows up.

Seven forty-eight. The bus barely clearing the corner.

I'm already outside.

"You're steady?" she asks.

"Yes."

She studies my face like she's reading weather patterns.

"Dim."

I compress instinctively.

The warmth folds inward without resistance.

Rowan nods once.

"Good."

We drive in silence.

Not awkward. Not tense.

Intentional.

The storefront looks worse in daylight.

Paper layered thick over the windows from the inside. Yellowed. Curling at the edges. The kind of place most people would assume closed ten years ago and never question.

Rowan parks in one of the slanted spaces directly in front.

Up close, the air feels different.

Warmer.

Denser.

Like the building itself is breathing.

Rowan steps to the door and places her palm flat against the wood.

The hum in my chest answers before I can stop it.

"Dim," she says, softly.

I compress again.

The paper over the windows ripple.

Not from wind.

From within.

Layer by layer, it begins to curl inward — not tearing, not falling — dissolving like it was never meant to be permanent.

Light pushes through.

Golden.

Not harsh like fluorescent lights.

Not white like midday sun.

Older.

The door unlocks without a sound.

Rowan opens it.

We step through.

The sound changes first.

"Did anyone outside see that?" I whisper to Rowan.

"No," says Rowan, in a whisper I can barely hear.

Above is the noise of engines, distant horns, and shopping carts.

Below sounds like wind through leaves.

Metal striking metal somewhere far off.

Voices layered over one another— bargaining, laughing, calling out prices.

When my eyes adjust, my breath leaves me.

Stone buildings line a narrow cobblestone street. Ivy climbs the walls. Ancient trees rise through the square, roots breaking the ground without apology. Sunlight pours from a sky that is too blue, too warm, as if it has existed longer than the one above.

It doesn't move the way normal sun moves.

It just … is.

Witches fill the square.

Openly.

No dimming.

Long skirts brushing stone. Boots. Sleeves rolled over tattooed forearms. Cauldrons stacked outside shop doors. Bundles of drying herbs hanging from iron hooks. Glass jars filled with eyeballs and powders that shimmer faintly when the light catches them.

And creatures.

A cat the size of a fox stretches across a windowsill, molten-gold eyes tracking every movement.

An owl perches on a wrought-iron hook and blinks sideways, feathers almost metallic in the sun.

Something small and horned—rabbit-sized but shaped wrong—darts across the street, fur trailing like smoke.

A broom sweeps a shop's front step by itself.

No one reacts.

No one stares.

This is ordinary here.

Wonder hits me so hard I almost laugh.

"It's beautiful," I whisper.

Rowan watches me instead of the square.

"Yes."

The air feels heavier here.

Not oppressive.

Anchored.

Like every breath carries memory.

A woman walks past carrying a crate of herbs. She doesn't stare, but her eyes flick to me once— measuring.

Recognition hums under my skin.

I don't know how I know this place.

But I do.

Paper cannot hide what blood will recognize.

A shop door opens across the square and the scent of sage and smoke rolls out. Two witches argue over the price of something glowing faintly blue in a vial. A child runs past holding a creature that looks like a ferret with folded wings pressed to its sides.

It's bustling.

Alive.

Controlled chaos.

And none of it feels evil.

That's what unsettles me most. I expected to sense evil and witches to be dressed in cloaks like you see on TV.

Rowan steps closer.

"They know you're here," she says, quietly.

I swallow.

"How?"

"You crossed."

As if summoned by the word, the hum in my chest shifts.

Not warmth.

Not anger.

Awareness.

Across the square, near the edge of a shaded alley, a woman stands still.

No stall.

No wares.

No movement.

Just watching.

She's not the woman from the grocery store.

Different face.

Same stillness.

Her head tilts slightly.

Acknowledgment.

Not threat.

Not yet.

Rowan's voice drops.

"Do not flare."

"I'm not."

"Good."

The woman turns and disappears into the alley without urgency.

Like she saw what she needed to see.

My pulse doesn't spike.

It settles.

That's worse.

"Welcome," says Rowan, softly, "to Below."

The word doesn't feel like a place.

It feels like a beginning.

And as I stand there in the golden light of a world I was never supposed to see, I understand something in my bones.

This isn't invasion.

It's return.

And somewhere beyond the square, beyond the shops and the creatures and the old stone buildings, someone else just felt me step inside.

Not curious.

Not surprised.

Interested.

The sun above doesn't move.

But something shifts.

And I know, without anyone saying it—

I was always going to come back.

Chapter
- 19 -
Mara

Rowan steers me toward a narrow shop tucked between a stone bakery and a stall selling

iron tools that hum faintly when touched.

A small brass bell hangs over the apothecary door.

It doesn't ring when we enter.

Inside, the air smells strong of dried herbs muddled together and something bitter I can't place.

Shelves line the walls from floor to ceiling, packed with jars and bundles and wrapped parcels tied with twine. Light filters through high windows, warm and steady.

An older woman stands behind the counter, sorting small green leaves into careful piles.

She looks up.

Her gaze lands on Rowan first.

Then me.

Something flickers in her eyes.

Not fear.

Recognition.

Rowan steps closer to a display of dried roots.

"This," she says quietly, picking one up, "is grounding. You use it when your pulse runs ahead of your control."

I reach for it.

It hums faintly in my fingers.

Not loud.

Not hot.

Steady.

"What do you do with it?" I ask.

"You can steep it or burn it," Rowan replies. "But only in small amounts."

The shop feels calm.

Safe.

For the first time since stepping through the door, my shoulders drop.

Maybe this is manageable.

Maybe Below isn't something to brace against.

The air shifts.

Not dramatically.

Just a degree cooler.

The woman behind the counter stills.

The steady hum of the square outside lowers by a fraction, like someone adjusted the volume on the world.

The door opens.

The bell does not ring.

I don't turn immediately.

I feel it first.

Not warmth.

Not anger.

Presence.

Deliberate.

Measured.

When I do look, she's already inside.

No cloak.

No theatrics.

Dark coat tailored sharp. Hair pulled back tight. Hands bare at her sides.

She is not beautiful in a soft way.

She is precise.

The kind of woman who wastes nothing— not words, nor movement.

Her eyes settle on me.

Not surprised.

Not curious.

Assessing.

The shopkeeper drops her gaze instantly.

Rowan goes very still beside me.

I don't know how I know this, but I do:

This is her.

Marlene.

Mara.

She steps closer.

One pace.

Enough that the golden light from the doorway brushes her face.

Her expression does not change.

She studies me like she's reading a document.

Then, quietly—

"You have Sebastian's eyes."

That name instantly takes my breath away.

My father.

My chest tightens.

She doesn't look at Rowan.

Doesn't acknowledge the shopkeeper.

Doesn't smile.

Doesn't explain.

Rowan's hand clamps around my arm.

"We're leaving."

Not loud.

Not panicked.

Final.

She drops coins on the counter without looking and pulls me toward the door.

I don't resist.

I don't speak.

I don't look back.

The sunlight in the square feels different now.

Not colder.

Sharper.

We cross the cobblestones quickly.

No one stops us.

No one intervenes.

And I can feel it—

Mara does not follow.

She doesn't need to.

The threshold swallows us in a rush of warm air and paper and silence.

When we step back onto the sidewalk Above, traffic roars like nothing happened.

Rowan doesn't release my arm until we're in the car.

Neither of us speaks.

But Sebastian's name echoes louder than anything I saw Below.

And for the first time in my life, my father's death doesn't feel like collateral damage.

It feels personal.

Chapter
- 20 -
Defiance

owan doesn't speak until we're three blocks away.

The engine hums steady. Traffic flows like nothing happened.

I stare out the windshield.

"She said his name."

Rowan's hands stay firm on the wheel.

"Yes."

"She remembered him."

"Yes."

That shouldn't feel like a punch.

But it does.

"The journal said he wasn't the target."

"He wasn't," Rowan replies.

My throat tightens anyway.

"But she looked at me like he mattered. Like he mattered to her."

Rowan's jaw shifts slightly.

"He did."

The words land heavier than anything else she's said.

Silence settles again, thick but not fragile.

"She let me believe it was an accident," I say.

"Your Grandma Dorothy let you be a child," Rowan replies.

That one splits something open.

A tear escapes before I can stop it. I wipe it away quickly, annoyed with myself.

"She lied."

"She carried it," corrects Rowan, evenly. "She carried it so you wouldn't have to."

I look at her then.

"You knew."

Rowan nods once.

"I knew what she was protecting."

"And you didn't tell me."

"It wasn't my story to tell," she says. Not defensive. Not apologetic. Certain.

I lean back in the seat.

"She didn't trust me."

"She trusted your future," Rowan says. "Dorothy understood consequences better than most of us."

That does something to my chest.

Warmth, gratitude, and anger all braided together.

"She looked at me like I belonged to her," I whisper.

Rowan's gaze flicks to me.

"You do. By blood."

I swallow.

"But blood doesn't decide allegiance."

There it is.

The line between inheritance and choice.

The car slows at a red light.

"She's not done," I say.

"No," Rowan agrees.

The light turns green.

"She expected me to be afraid," I say.

Rowan doesn't answer that.

Because she doesn't need to.

I sit with the echo of Sebastian's name in my head. My father's name.

With Grandma Dorothy's silence reframed as protection.

With Mara's measured stare.

And something inside me settles into place.

Not fear.

Not rage.

Resolve.

Rowan's voice is quiet when she speaks again.

"Blood doesn't disappear, Izzy. It waits."

I wipe the last trace of moisture from my cheek.

"I'm not waiting."

Rowan glances at me.

No warning this time.

No lecture.

Just recognition.

And somewhere Below, in a square of old stone and unmoving sun, Mara feels the shift.

Not fear.

Not retreat.

Interest.

Her granddaughter did not leave shaken.

She left awake.

Chapter
- 21 -
Reinforcement

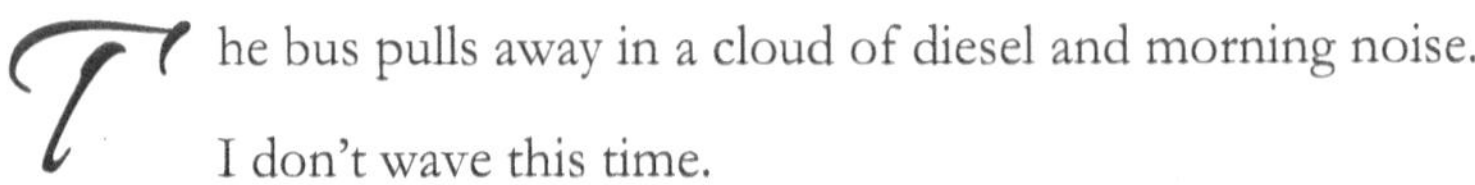

The bus pulls away in a cloud of diesel and morning noise.

I don't wave this time.

I just stand there until it turns the corner.

Then I go back inside.

The house is quiet.

Not heavy.

Not wrong.

Aware.

The journal is open on the kitchen table.

I know I closed it.

The page isn't frantic.

No ink bleeding.

No dramatic script.

One word.

Reinforce.

That's it.

Below it—

Salt each doorway.

Iron above thresholds.

Mark the hearth.

Hang what holds.

No explanation.

No warning.

Just instruction.

I don't argue.

I don't question.

I go to the cabinet and pull down the salt.

I walk to the front door first.

Not the back.

Not the attic.

The front.

I pour a thin line across the threshold. Slow. Even.

Not messy.

Intentional.

The house doesn't flare.

It settles.

I move to the side door.

Then the door to the garage.

Each one.

Slowly.

When I return to the front door, I stop.

The horseshoe hangs exactly where it always has.

Upside down.

Decorative.

Southern.

Unremarkable.

Except it isn't.

It never was.

Grandma Dorothy didn't believe in luck.

She believed in structure.

I touch the iron lightly.

Cold.

Steady.

Holding.

I leave it where it is.

Next—

Iron.

My mind snaps back to the horseshoe. Then, to the nails we bought Below.

The ones that hummed faintly in my palm.

Three above each doorway.

Not visible.

Not announced.

Hidden strength.

The hammer strikes are quiet.

Measured.

With each nail, something in the house tightens and steadies.

Like a spine aligning.

When I finish the last threshold, I walk to the kitchen and instinctively grab a small knife. Then I approach the fireplace with purpose.

The symbol on my hand burns faintly in memory.

Not pain.

Recognition.

I kneel.

Press the blade into the wood beam above the hearth.

Carve.

Not large.

Not ornate.

Exact.

When the final line connects—

The air shifts.

Not violently.

Just enough.

Like the house inhales and decides to remain standing.

Lavender sits on the counter.

The bundles from the apothecary.

I hang them above the back door.

Fresh.

Not decorative.

Purposeful.

I step back.

Look at the room.

Nothing looks different.

And yet—

Everything feels anchored.

I don't feel afraid.

I don't feel reactive.

I feel—

Stronger.

Safer.

Not because nothing can touch me.

Because I understand the rules.

And I am playing by them.

Now Below—

In a square of old stone and unmoving sun, Mara stills mid-conversation.

It reaches her quietly.

Salt at the thresholds.

Iron driven above the doors.

A mark carved at the hearth.

Something in her face tightens.

Even in death, she interferes.

A flicker of irritation moves through her— sharp, immediate.

"Fucking Dorothy," she says.

Not loud.

Not emotional.

Measured.

She exhales slowly.

Of course, the house was reinforced.

Of course, instruction was left behind.

She never relied on hope.

She relied on structure.

Mara's gaze shifts slightly.

The granddaughter did not panic.

She reinforced.

That is … inconvenient.

And interesting.

The board shifts.

Not dramatically.

But enough.

And somewhere Above the child is not hiding.

She's preparing.

Chapter
- 22 -
Pressure

The farmer's market is louder than it should be.

Live music plays near the bakery tent.

Children weave between tables.

Someone argues over the price of heirloom tomatoes.

Maddie is holding a bundle of sunflowers like she's about to propose to someone.

"Please," I say, scanning a display of local honey. "Let today just be tomatoes and sourdough."

Rowan's mouth twitches faintly. "You live dangerously."

I almost laugh.

Then the air changes.

Not visibly.

Not dramatically.

Just—

Pressure.

It tightens around my ribs like someone pulled a cord through my spine. The breeze stops moving the tent fabric. The music dulls, as if it's underwater.

No one else reacts.

A woman at the next table keeps sampling peaches.

A child drops a strawberry and cries.

"There are watchers here," says Rowan, quietly.

Three men stand at separate stalls.

Too still.

Too aware.

Not shopping.

Watching.

The pressure builds.

Not heat.

Not light.

Containment.

Like something is trying to fold inward around me.

One of them shifts.

Another takes a step.

The third raises his hand slightly.

The air tightens.

My lungs strain.

And then— a shift.

Subtle.

Precise.

Like altitude correcting by a single degree.

The weight drops instantly.

The raised hand falters.

All three men freeze.

Not because of me.

Because of him.

He steps forward from the space between two tents.

Not flashy.

Not theatrical.

Just present.

Tall.

Tan skin catching the afternoon light.

Blue eyes are steady and unreadable.

He moves one half-step in front of me. His arm comes back slightly, not touching, just shielding the space behind him.

A barrier.

Controlled.

To anyone else, it looks like a man adjusting his position in a crowded market.

But the air feels different.

Corrected.

He doesn't look at me first.

He looks at them.

Measured.

Deliberate.

Hierarchy.

Then he turns.

Our eyes meet.

Not lingering.

Not soft.

Just— recognition.

Something in him recalibrates.

He wasn't expecting that.

His voice is low.

Even.

"Go. Now," Rowan says.

Her hand clamps around my arm.

We move.

Maddie stumbles slightly, confused but following.

No one shouts.

No one follows.

The market noise swallows us whole.

Halfway to the parking lot, I look back.

He's still standing there.

Watching.

Not the watchers.

Me.

Then he turns away first.

Controlled.

The air feels normal again.

But my pulse doesn't.

Blue eyes.

Tan skin.

Rugged jaw.

Control.

And for one impossible second—

I felt steady.

Safe.

Chapter
- 23 -
Intervention

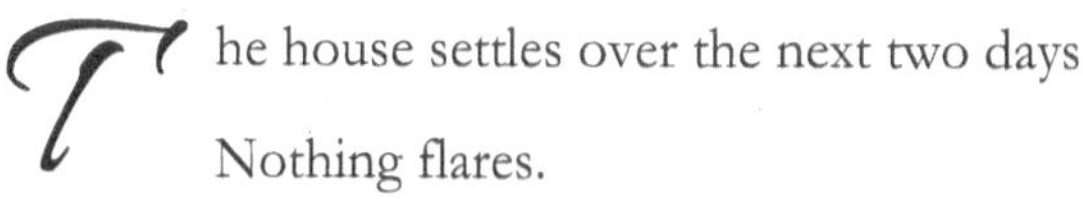

The house settles over the next two days.

Nothing flares.

Nothing knocks.

I almost start to believe it worked.

Then Rowan texts one word.

Now.

No punctuation. No warmth.

I stare at the screen like it might change its mind.

It doesn't.

The house feels different.

Held.

Standing a little straighter.

Reinforced.

I grab my keys anyway.

Because reinforced doesn't mean untouchable.

It means I'm done pretending.

Rowan is already in my driveway when I step outside.

She lowers the window.

"You steady?"

"Yes."

Her eyes sweep over me, quick and clinical.

"Dim."

I compress.

The warmth folds inward cleanly, obedient.

Rowan nods once.

"Good. Get in."

No small talk.

We drive in silence.

The closer we get, the more my body pays attention.

Not fear.

Recognition.

The storefront waits like it did before.

Paper yellowed and curled over the windows.

Rowan parks.

"One rule," she says.

I almost smile. "Only one?"

"Do not flare."

"I won't."

She studies me one more beat.

Then we step toward the door.

Her palm meets wood.

The hum answers inside my chest.

I dim hard.

The paper ripples.

Layer by layer, it dissolves.

Golden light spills through.

We step Below.

I hear the sounds again, first.

Wind through leaves.

Metal striking metal somewhere distant.

Voices bargaining like it's market day and not another world.

Then the square unfolds.

Stone buildings.

Ivy climbing over cracked stone walls.

Ancient trees breaking through cobblestone without apology.

That unmoving sun.

Witches move openly.

Cauldrons are stacked near doorways.

Herbs hanging in dense, fragrant bundles and creatures. Wild, amazing creatures.

Scaled lizards no longer than a pinky finger perch on warm stone, throats pulsing faintly violet. A small sign reads: Heat-fed. Do not touch.

A stall displays three smooth, charcoal-colored eggs on a bed of ash. Another sign reads: Dragon eggs. Handle at your own risk.

A pair of massive owls sit on carved wooden stands, feathers-streaked silver and midnight blue, eyes luminous and unblinking.

Something with too many joints skitters up a wall and vanishes into the ivy.

Nobody reacts.

This is ordinary here.

Maddie inhales dramatically. "If I come home with a dragon, mind your business."

Rowan ignores her.

"We're not sightseeing," she says. "Books first."

We move toward a narrow bookstore tucked between a bakery and a stall selling ironwork that hums faintly when touched.

Inside, shelves rise from floor to ceiling.

Rowan moves with precision.

"These," she says, pulling two leather-bound volumes from a shelf. "Protection. Containment. Structural magic. You'll need to read them."

I take them carefully.

She reaches for a smaller book.

"And this," she says. "Your journal."

I look at her.

All witches keep one," she says, evenly. "Spells. Thoughts. Mistakes."

I hug the stack of books against my chest. "Do I get a wand or something cool, or is it just homework?"

Maddie snorts.

Rowan looks at me like I just asked for a tiara.

"Read," she says.

Maddie wanders toward a display of charms. "And ideas you pretend weren't your idea later, that's what's in my journal!"

I almost laugh.

Then, I see it.

A black kitten curled in a shallow, wooden crate near the counter.

Small.

Still.

Gold eyes half-open, watching.

Drawn is not a strong enough word.

I kneel before I realize I've moved.

The kitten blinks slowly.

Rowan's voice comes from behind me.

"If you take it, it's yours for life."

I don't look away from the eyes.

"For life?"

"Guardian cats bind to one person," Rowan says. "They protect who they choose."

The kitten stands.

Walks directly toward me.

Maddie makes a quiet sound. "Well. That seems decided."

I swallow.

"I'll take her."

Rowan studies the cat once, then nods.

"Good."

The kitten settles into my duffle bag like it's been waiting for me.

And then—

The air tightens.

No sound.

No movement.

Pressure.

Rowan's shoulders go rigid.

I turn.

Three watchers stand at the edge of the narrow passage outside the shop.

Spaced.

Deliberate.

A dark-haired woman with eyes that measure too closely.

A man in a heavy coat despite the warm sun.

And a younger one whose stillness feels rehearsed.

"She crosses again," the woman says.

"She's allowed," Rowan replies.

"Allowed by who?"

"Balance."

The younger one smiles faintly.

The pressure builds.

Not heat.

Containment.

The younger watcher's fingers move slightly, almost lazy.

The air constricts around my lungs.

Rowan grips my wrist.

"Dim," she says, quietly.

"I am," I answer through gritted teeth.

The pressure increases.

Testing.

The younger watcher tilts his head.

"She's loud."

Rowan's voice sharpens. "Enough."

He doesn't stop.

The air compresses harder.

My vision narrows.

And then— a shift.

Precise.

Controlled.

The pressure collapses instantly.

Like it never existed.

Someone steps between us.

Tall.

Broad shoulders.

Tan skin catching the gold light.

Blue eyes are steady and unreadable.

He doesn't look at me.

He looks at them.

His arm slides behind me—across my back—shielding without touching.

A boundary drawn.

"That's enough," he says.

The younger watcher stiffens. "This isn't your—"

The blue-eyed man turns his head slightly.

The sentence dies.

"We were instructed to watch," the woman says.

"And instructed not to harm her," he replies.

Calm.

Final.

The younger watcher bristles. "She isn't harmed."

The blue-eyed man lifts one hand, effortlessly.

The remaining tension dissolves completely.

Gone.

Rowan exhales once.

Small.

Tight.

Only then does he turn.

His gaze meets mine.

Measured.

Assessing.

Something recalibrates behind his eyes.

Not softness.

Not surprise.

Recognition.

He wasn't expecting that.

"Go," he says.

Rowan doesn't hesitate.

She catches my wrist and pulls.

We move through the square without running.

No one stops us.

The storefront swallows us whole.

Warm air.

Paper.

Then— Above.

Traffic.

Engines.

Noise.

Rowan releases my wrist as she unlocks the car.

We get inside.

Doors are shut.

Her breathing stays steady.

Too steady.

"He stepped in front of me," I say.

"Yes."

"He stopped them."

"Yes."

I look at her.

"Who is he?"

Rowan starts the engine.

"We're not talking about him yet."

The car pulls away.

But my body is still in that alley.

Still feeling the shift.

Still hearing the command.

Go.

I don't know his name.

But I know this— he wasn't supposed to intervene.

And he did.

Below, the report is delivered without drama.

The watcher who cast the pressure spell keeps his gaze lowered.

The blue-eyed man stands still.

Dimmed clean.

"You were given strict orders," says Mara, evenly.

Silence.

She turns to him.

"Alaric."

Acknowledgment. Rank.

"You followed instructions."

Approval, sharp as steel.

"Effective."

His expression does not change.

"New assignment," Mara continues.

"Watch her. Stay close. Report directly to me."

A pause.

Alaric nods.

Then, quieter—

"Fucking Dorothy."

Her eyes narrow slightly.

"The girl is not hiding."

A faint curve touches her mouth.

"She's preparing."

Chapter
- 24 -
Unfinished

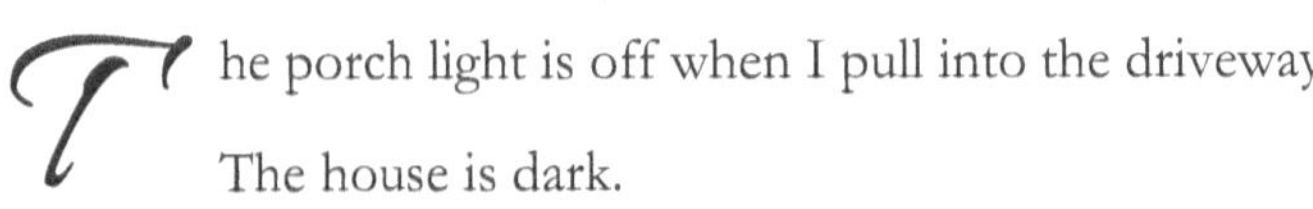

The porch light is off when I pull into the driveway.

The house is dark.

Quiet.

Safe.

I shut the car door maybe a little louder than necessary and steady myself against the hood for half a second.

I'm not drunk.

Just … warm.

Ladies' night did exactly what it was supposed to do. Whew. I am relaxed.

I climb the porch steps.

And stop.

Someone is sitting on the top step.

Still.

Silent.

My heart punches once, hard.

Then he leans forward into the faint wash of streetlight.

Blue eyes.

Calm.

Of course.

"You're going to give me a heart attack," I say, pressing a hand to my chest.

"You asked for trust," he replies, evenly.

I narrow my eyes.

"You lurking in the shadows counts as trust now?"

"I was not lurking."

"You were absolutely lurking."

His gaze drifts over me once— slow, assessing.

"It appears you enjoyed your evening."

I blink at him.

"Were you at the bar?"

"I was nearby."

I laugh under my breath.

"That's not creepy at all."

He does not react.

That makes it worse.

I take one more step up so I'm standing directly in front of him.

"You shouldn't be here," I tell him.

And I tap his chest lightly with my index finger.

He doesn't move.

Doesn't flinch.

Just looks down at my hand like it's an interesting development.

"Not like this," he says.

"But you are."

The edges of my words blur just slightly.

Not sloppy.

Just honest.

The step shifts faintly under my heel when I lean in.

I wobble.

Just a fraction.

His hand comes up instantly.

Firm around my waist.

Steady.

My palms land against his chest to catch myself.

Solid.

Warm.

We are suddenly very close.

Too close.

He doesn't let go immediately.

Neither of us pretend that was entirely accidental.

"You should stand carefully," he says, quietly.

"I'm standing just fine," I say.

I don't move away.

I tilt my chin up instead.

"You could have let them hurt me."

"No," he answers immediately.

No hesitation.

No calculation.

Just truth.

That does something to me.

I step even closer.

Close enough that our breaths mix.

"You don't look like a man who enjoys reporting," I say, softly.

"I do not."

"Then why do you?"

"Because order matters."

"So does choice," I whisper.

For the first time, something shifts in his expression.

Conflict.

Not softness.

Not yet.

But real.

His hand slides from my waist to the small of my back.

Not pulling.

Just there.

A boundary.

A warning.

"You are less guarded tonight," he says.

"Maybe I'm tired of guarding."

My fingers curl lightly in the fabric of his shirt.

"You are…" he starts.

The words hang there.

Unfinished.

I smile slowly.

"I am what?"

His jaw tightens.

"You are—"

He stops.

Something vulnerable flickers across his face.

I lean closer.

So close my lips nearly brush his.

"Say it."

His grip tightens at my back.

For one suspended second, I am certain he's going to kiss me.

Instead— he pulls back just enough to breathe.

"You are drunk," he says, evenly.

I stare at him.

"That's the word you picked?"

His mouth almost curves.

"You should go inside."

"You almost said something else."

He doesn't deny it.

Doesn't confirm it.

He just studies me like I am something dangerous.

"You are not as careful as you believe yourself to be," he says.

"And you," I counter, "are not as cold as you pretend."

That lands.

Hard.

He steps back first.

Because if he doesn't, he won't.

"I will remain nearby," he says.

Of course he will.

I hold his gaze one second longer.

Then I turn and unlock the door.

Ionder if he's going to follow me in.

My fingers fumble slightly with the key.

I blame the drinks.

Not the way my pulse won't slow down.

The lock clicks.

I glance back.

I was just about to ask him his name—

but he's gone.

No sound.

No flash.

Just absence.

I close the door softly behind me.

Lean against it.

The house is quiet.

Safe.

Normal.

My pulse is not.

I lift my fingers slowly to my waist.

The exact spot where his hand had been.

Still warm.

Still steady.

"You are—"

I close my eyes.

"You are what?" I say under my breath.

What the hell was he about to say?

I wasn't drunk.

He was lying.

I know he was lying.

I push away from the door and walk down the hall.

Halfway to the stairs I stop.

Turn.

Like I expect him to still be there.

Watching.

He isn't.

Of course he isn't.

When I finally crawl into bed, sleep doesn't come quickly.

Every time I close my eyes, I see him.

Feel his hand at my back.

Hear the unfinished word hanging between us.

You are—

I roll onto my side and stare into the dark.

"This is going to be a problem," I whisper.

And I don't want it to be.

Chapter
- 25 -
Confession

I wake up with regret.

Not emotional regret.

Hydration regret.

My mouth tastes like bad decisions and lime.

I stare at the ceiling for a full ten seconds before rolling onto my side and squinting at the clock.

Too early.

My head throbs once in protest.

"Fantastic," I say.

Every time I close my eyes—

Him.

His hand at my back.

"You are—"

I groan and roll onto my other side.

Nope.

Not doing this before coffee.

By the time I get the girls out the door, my head is pounding and my patience is thin.

Lily looks suspiciously observant.

Rose is blissfully twelve.

"Mom, you okay?" asks Lily, as she slings her backpack on.

I blink at her.

"Fine."

She studies me for half a second longer than necessary.

Structure.

Just like Rowan.

The bus pulls away.

The house falls quiet.

I walk inside, close the door, and immediately grab my phone.

Me: Come over.

Me: Boy, do I have some tea for you.

Three dots appear almost instantly.

Maddie: If this is about Blue Eyes I am already on my way.

Maddie: Do I bring pastries or bail money?

I snort.

Me: Just you. Now. Hurry.

Maddie walks in like she pays rent — sunglasses on, oversized sweater, zero shame.

"You look like someone who made questionable choices," she says.

"I made choices."

She drops into the kitchen chair and leans forward.

"Tell me everything."

I pour coffee. Strong. Aggressive.

"He was on my porch."

Her mouth drops open.

"Excuse me?"

"Just sitting there. Like he lives here."

She slaps the table.

"Stop."

"I'm serious."

"Was he brooding?"

"Yes."

"Did he look unfairly good in low lighting?"

"Yes."

She grips her mug dramatically.

"This is my Super Bowl."

I roll my eyes, but I'm smiling.

"He said I was less guarded."

"Ooooh."

"And then he almost said something."

Her entire body stills.

"Almost?"

"He started with 'You are—' and then stopped."

Maddie gasps like I just told her someone proposed.

"WHAT."

"I leaned in."

"You did not."

"I did."

"How close?"

"Close."

"Like kissing close?"

"Like breathing the same air close."

She makes a strangled noise.

"And?"

"He said I was drunk."

The silence is immediate.

Maddie stares at me.

"That coward."

"I know."

"He was absolutely about to say something."

"He was."

"What was it?"

"I don't know!"

I run a hand through my hair.

"You are what?" I say again. "What was he about to say?"

Maddie leans back in her chair, eyes gleaming.

"He's in trouble."

"I'm in trouble."

She points at me.

"No. You are glowing."

"I am hungover."

"You are glowing and hungover."

I try not to smile.

Fail.

"He caught me when I stumbled," I admit.

Her jaw drops again.

"Hand placement?"

"Waist."

"OH MY GOD."

"It was very steady."

"Of course it was steady. He's disciplined and tortured and sexy."

"I hate that you're right."

She narrows her eyes.

"Did he look at your mouth?"

"Yes."

"Did you look at his?"

"Yes."

She slams her hand on the table again.

"This is not casual."

"I know."

We sit on that for a second.

Then Maddie leans forward, voice lowering slightly.

"Be careful."

There it is.

The shift.

"I know," I say quietly.

"He reports to her."

"I know."

"But he didn't have to step in."

"No."

"And he didn't have to show up on your porch."

"No."

We lock eyes.

"He likes you," says Maddie, simply.

I swallow.

"He shouldn't."

"Well, that's too bad for him."

I stare into my coffee.

"We can't tell Rowan."

Maddie barks out a laugh.

"Absolutely not."

"She will shit bricks!"

"Then she will build a fortress out of those bricks and lock you in it." Maddie says.

We both laugh.

Then Maddie points at me again.

"Do not tell Rowan yet."

"I wasn't planning on it."

"Good."

She squints at me.

"You're going to see him again."

It's not a question.

I hesitate.

"…Probably. He's fucking following me, Maddie."

She nods slowly.

"Okay."

"Okay?"

"Okay."

"That's it?"

"No," she says, lifting her mug. "That's me deciding I want front row seats."

I laugh.

But underneath it, something steadier settles.

This is reckless.

Complicated.

Dangerous.

And I already know—

if he shows up again,

I'm going to make him finish that sentence.

Chapter
- 26 -
Temptation

The house is quiet.

The girls are asleep.

Ten acres of dark stretch beyond the porch like the world ends at my fence line.

I light the joint with hands steadier than I feel.

Rowan's warning still lingers in my bones.

Do not invite complication.

Smoke curls into the warm night air.

"You are attempting to relax."

I don't turn.

"Do you ever knock?"

"I do not need to."

I glance over my shoulder.

He steps from shadow into the low porch light.

Blue eyes.

Steady.

Watching.

"You're getting bold," I say, softly.

"I am assigned."

I turn toward him fully. "Assigned?"

"I am meant to watch you. And report."

The honesty of it hits harder than it should.

"Then report this," I say, stepping closer.

He doesn't retreat.

That's his mistake.

I close the distance myself.

"If you're going to follow me," I say, tapping his chest lightly with my finger, "at least stop pretending it's only duty."

His hand catches my wrist.

Firm.

Warm.

Intentional.

"You do not understand what you are inviting."

"Then explain it."

That's when he moves.

Fast.

His hand grips my waist and lifts me onto the porch railing in one smooth motion. The joint falls somewhere behind us, forgotten.

He steps between my knees.

Solid.

Close.

Heat radiating through thin fabric.

His mouth crashes into mine.

Deep.

Not cautious.

Not restrained.

It's hunger finally given permission.

I pull him closer by his shirt. He groans low against my mouth — a sound that makes my pulse spike.

His hands slide up the back of my shirt, fingers spreading against my skin before tightening at my waist.

My breath stutters when his mouth leaves mine and trails along my jaw… down the side of my neck.

Slow.

Intentional.

His voice rough against my skin.

"Isobel."

"It's Izzy," I whisper, arching slightly toward him.

His fingers tighten.

"You are—" he begins.

I pull back just enough to look at him.

"I am what?"

His eyes drag over me.

Not just desire.

Something deeper.

Almost stunning.

"You are beautiful," he says.

Not polished.

Not detached.

Like it costs him something to admit.

The word warms my chest and spreads outward.

He exhales sharply — like he shouldn't have said it.

Like he already regrets how honest he was.

My shirt shifts beneath his hands.

Fabric strains.

Buttons give way under sudden pressure as he grabs the front of my blouse and pulls it open.

Cool night air meets warm skin.

His breathing changes instantly.

Rougher.

Less controlled.

His gaze lowers—reverent, almost disbelieving—like the sight of me unsettles him more than touching me ever could.

His mouth returns to my throat.

Lower.

Slower.

His hands grip my waist harder as his lips trace a deliberate path down the center of my neck … across warm skin … lingering.

My head tips back against the porch post.

His mouth follows the curve of my collarbone.

Lower still.

Heat spreads through me in waves.

My fingers are tangled into his hair, guiding him without thinking.

He exhales against my skin—not steady anymore.

Not disciplined.

For a moment, he forgets everything.

The porch.

The assignment.

Mara.

Order.

It's just breath and hands and heat and the way his mouth moves over me like he's memorizing something forbidden.

And then he stills.

Not because he wants to.

Because he must.

He pulls back abruptly.

Breathing heavier than I've ever seen him.

His hands remain at my waist a second longer before releasing.

His eyes meet mine.

Shaken.

Not by what we did.

By what he feels.

"This is not wise," he says, voice tight.

I give him a slow, breathless smile.

"You're the one who showed up."

His jaw flexes.

"That was my first mistake."

He steps back as if discipline is snapping back into place piece by piece.

"I am meant to watch you," he says quietly again. "And report."

"And are you?" I ask.

A pause.

Too long.

His hand rises to my cheek one last time.

Gentler now.

"I will ensure you are safe," he says instead.

Not answering.

But answering.

He leans in again.

This kiss is different.

Slower.

Intentional.

Less frantic.

A claim.

Not a loss of control.

When he pulls away, he looks at me like leaving costs him something real.

Then he steps back into shadow.

And he's gone.

I sit on the railing, shirt open, skin warm in the night air.

Ten acres of silence.

My heart still racing.

Rowan told me not to invite complication.

Too late.

He isn't cold.

He isn't detached.

And I just watched a disciplined man lose control because of me.

Fuck.

Chapter
- 27 -
Inheritance

The movie is halfway through and I have no idea what's happening.

Lily is beside me on the couch, thumbs moving like her life depends on whatever conversation is lighting up her phone.

Midnight is stretched across the back cushion like he's lived here for years.

For a moment, it almost feels normal.

Lily throws her phone down onto the couch.

The glass globe on the mantle explodes.

It doesn't fall.

It doesn't tip.

It shatters.

Glass rains down across the hardwood in a violent spray.

I dim instantly.

Hard.

Everything inside me compresses—tight and fast—scanning for threat.

My eyes sweep the room.

Windows.

Door.

Air.

Nothing.

Then I look at Lily.

She's frozen.

Midnight bolts upright— then leaps straight onto her lap.

Not mine.

Hers.

She flinches at the impact, then wraps her arms around him.

And the sob breaks out of her like it's been waiting.

I'm on my knees in front of her before I register moving.

"Hey. Hey." My voice stays even. "Look at me."

She shakes her head, crying harder.

"I didn't mean to. I didn't mean to."

"Lily." I take her wrists gently. "Has this happened before?"

She hesitates.

That's my answer.

Tears streak down her face.

"The vase," she whispers. "Grandma's vase. It wasn't Midnight. I did it. I just— I got mad and it just—"

Her hands flex unconsciously.

"I think something is wrong with me, Mom."

I feel that deep in my soul.

"There is nothing wrong with you," I say, immediately.

She swallows.

Then she wipes her face with the heel of her palm and turns her hand slightly into the light from the window.

"Mom?"

I look down.

The mark sits faint beneath her skin.

Not bright. Not loud. Just a thin fracture of molten light— precise and ancient. Unmistakable.

My breath stops.

I know it instantly.

My stomach drops anyway.

Lily watches my face carefully.

"You know what it is."

Not accusation.

Hope.

I don't answer right away.

I turn my own hand into the sunlight.

The same mark gleams faintly under my skin.

Lily exhales.

Her shoulders drop a bit.

Relief.

I give her a reassuring smile.

"I'll explain everything," I say, quietly.

"Remember the chairs I donated?" Lily nods.

"I didn't donate them; I slammed them into each other." I admit, clearly ashamed of myself.

"I need to show you something, get up."

In the kitchen, I place a sugar packet on the counter between us.

Lily's eyes flick from the packet to me.

I dim.

Slow.

Intentional.

The packet slides cleanly into my palm.

No strain.

No spectacle.

Just control.

Her mouth parts slightly.

"You're not broken," I say.

Her spine straightens.

"Okay," she whispers.

"I'm glad Rose is at a sleepover tonight," I say, more to myself than to her.

Because this? This would be a lot for a twelve-year-old.

"Get your shoes," I say. "We're going to see Rowan."

Rowan opens the door before I knock.

Her eyes go straight to Lily.

Then to me.

"What happened?" she asks.

"Globe. Vase. And this."

Lily steps forward and holds out her hand.

Rowan takes it without hesitation.

Studies the mark.

No shock.

No flare.

Just assessment.

"When did it appear?"

"The night the vase broke like three days ago," says Lily, quietly.

Rowan nods once.

"All right."

That's it.

No drama.

We move to the kitchen table.

Rowan reaches into a drawer and places a small iron ring on the wood between us.

Lily looks at it.

I swallow.

"Iron resists," I say softly. "It's why we nail it above doors."

Rowan's eyes flick to mine briefly.

Then back to Lily.

"Do not push," Rowan says. "Do not grab. Call it."

Lily nods.

Serious.

Focused.

The ring trembles.

Then lifts.

Clean.

Three inches above the table.

Steady.

My breath catches.

Rowan's fingers still for a fraction of a second.

The ring holds.

Perfectly level.

Then Lily's eyes flick to Rowan.

The ring drops back to the table with a sharp metallic sound.

She blinks.

Looks at Rowan.

Then at me.

"Did I do it right?"

Rowan studies her.

"You were fire first," she says, quietly to me.

"She listens before she burns."

I'm not sure if that's praise.

Then Rowan looks at Lily again.

"Well-done."

Two words.

And I almost fall out of my chair.

Rowan slides the ring toward Lily.

"You will place this on your desk," she says, evenly.

"You will sit."

"You will not let it rise above your eye level."

"If it trembles, you lower it."

"Ten breaths."

"Every day."

"Seven days."

Lily nods once.

No fear now.

Just determination.

A quiet settles over the table.

I look at her.

Really look at her.

And something inside me loosens.

Not fear.

Not being overwhelmed.

Relief.

"I think…" I say slowly, almost to myself. "Grandma Dorothy would have called this inevitable."

Rowan doesn't contradict me.

Lily turns her head.

"Grandma knew?"

Not upset.

Not scared.

Curious.

I meet her eyes.

"She knew more than she ever said."

And for the first time since all this shit started—

I don't feel so alone in this.

"I don't know when my house turned into Hogwarts," I say out loud, "but apparently we're enrolling."

Rowan side-eyes me.

Lily does, too.

I lift my hands defensively.

"What? I cope with humor."

Silence.

Then Rowan continues like I never spoke.

"Power without steadiness is noise."

Lily absorbs that.

Nods again.

Below, Mara wakes abruptly.

Not from fear.

From steadiness.

In the fading edges of her dream, iron hung suspended.

Perfectly still.

She sits up slowly.

Tests the current.

Stronger.

Cleaner.

She closes her eyes again.

"She's learning," she murmurs into the dark.

Satisfied.

And lies back down.

Chapter
- 28 -
Ash and Iron

Below smells like iron and smoke.

Mara stands before a low stone table, fingers resting lightly on the rim of a shallow iron bowl filled with dark water. A thin silver thread runs from the bowl to her hand.

Across from her,a girl who looks no older than thirteen kneels.

Esther.

Small.

Soft-faced.

Harmless.

Her eyes are not.

"You will observe both children," says Mara, evenly.

Esther nods once.

"The elder has awakened. The younger remains innocent."

A faint smile curves Mara's mouth.

"Do not harm the innocent sister."

Esther's gaze sharpens.

"You will bring her Below."

The silver thread hums faintly between Mara's fingers.

"You will confirm Alaric's loyalty."

Esther tilts her head.

"And if he fails?"

"Then, I will know," replies Mara, calmly. "And he will be dealt with."

She slides a narrow blade across the stone.

The metal is dark, matte, absorbing light rather than reflecting it.

"The Veilblade opens one seam," Mara says. "No hesitation. No spectacle. Be swift."

Esther takes it carefully.

"And if the mother interferes?"

"She will." Mara's expression does not shift. "Do not kill her."

A beat.

"Do not underestimate her."

The silver thread tightens once.

"Go."

Esther smiles.

And vanishes.

Above, the house feels normal.

Too normal.

Rose chatters in the kitchen.

"She's really nice, Mom. She doesn't even go to school here. Her parents travel."

Izzy dries her hands on a towel.

"What's her name?"

"Esther."

Midnight, stretched along the windowsill, lifts his head.

A low hiss slips from his throat.

Izzy glances at him. "Midnight, stop."

Lily stiffens slightly beside the counter.

"Something's weird," she says.

The doorbell rings.

Esther is standing on the porch when Izzy opens the door.

Polite.

Still.

Too still.

"Hello, ma'am, I'm here to see Rose."

Her smile is perfect.

Her eyes slide briefly to Lily.

Then to Rose.

Rose grabs Esther's hand. "Come on! I'll show you my room!"

Midnight's fur rises along his spine.

Izzy feels it then.

A pressure shift.

Subtle.

Wrong.

"Rose—"

Too late.

The air splits.

Esther moves faster than a child should.

Her grip tightens on Rose's arm.

A thin vertical slit tears open the air beside them.

Darkness breathes outward.

Cold wind rushes into the house.

Rose screams.

Half her body vanishes into the seam.

Izzy lunges, grabbing Rose's legs.

"No!"

Lily's hands lift instinctively.

The iron above the door vibrates.

Esther's face shifts.

Not monstrous.

Just older.

Cold.

She angles the Veilblade toward Lily.

"You are not part of this assignment. Step back."

Lily doesn't step back.

She pushes.

Controlled.

Structured.

The seam wavers.

But Esther is stronger.

Rose's fingers claw at the hardwood.

"Mom!"

The pressure spikes—

And then it changes.

Alaric steps through the back doorway as if he's been standing in the shadows the entire time.

His eyes take in everything at once.

The Veilblade.

The seam.

Rose halfway through.

Esther sees him.

"Alaric."

Not greeting.

Confirmation.

He does not speak.

He moves.

One clean motion.

The blade drives beneath her ribs.

Precise.

Efficient.

Esther's breath leaves her with a soft, stunned sound.

The seam flickers violently.

Alaric rips the Veilblade free, shoves Esther's slack body fully through the slit, and pulls Rose back in the same movement.

The seam collapses.

Silence slams down.

Rose falls into Izzy's arms.

A red handprint burns faintly on her arm.

Then dulls.

Izzy gathers her daughter against her chest.

Tears spill before she can stop them.

Her hands shake for a moment.

Then she steadies.

Lily stands beside them, breathing hard but upright.

Alaric remains where he stands.

Blade in hand.

Controlled.

His eyes shift briefly to Lily.

He gives the smallest nod.

Precise. Acknowledging.

Then his focus returns to Izzy.

Izzy looks up at him.

He waits for recoil, but it doesn't come.

Rose goes limp in her arms.

Not unconscious.

Just spent.

Izzy presses her face into her daughter's hair.

Her voice is hoarse but steady when she speaks.

"I'm calling Rowan."

Chapter
- 29 -
Grounding

owan arrives within minutes.

Bag in hand.

Eyes scanning.

She doesn't ask what happened.

She sees it.

The faint scorch in the air where the seam tore.

The residue of Below clinging to the room.

Rose asleep against Izzy's shoulder.

Lily upright.

Unbroken.

And Alaric. The Veilblade still in his hand.

Rowan's gaze locks onto it.

"Give me the blade."

Not a question.

A command.

Alaric's fingers tighten around the hilt for half a breath.

Instinct.

He hands it over.

Rowan takes it without thanks or acknowledgment.

She wraps it immediately in a strip of iron-threaded cloth pulled from her bag and sets it aside.

Only then does she look at him fully.

"What did she use?" asks Rowan, though she already knows.

"Veilblade," Alaric answers.

Rowan nods once.

Of course.

She kneels by the coffee table and opens her bag.

Red fabric. Three by five inches.

An iron needle.

Red thread.

Her hands move quickly. Efficient. Controlled.

"Mugwort seals thresholds," she says as she begins sewing three sides of the small pouch. "Caraway keeps wandering spirits from clinging."

She drops in a snowflake obsidian stone.

"For grounding. For balance."

A measured pinch of salt.

"Iron remembers what crosses it."

She pulls the red yarn tight and knots it closed.

She hands the small bag to Izzy.

"Hang this above the outside of her bedroom door."

She makes two more without pause.

"Front door. Back door. They will not cross twice."

Her voice remains steady. Even now.

She reaches into the bag again.

Pink satin this time.

Softer.

Lavender.

Spearmint.

Violets.

A small measure of iron shavings.

Cotton batting to bind it all.

"This one quiets the mind," says Rowan, as she sews all four sides closed. "It keeps the doorways inside the head from reopening."

She slides it gently beneath Rose's pillow.

Rose's breathing deepens almost immediately.

Rowan places her hand over Rose's forehead.

Whispers words in a language Izzy does not recognize.

Low.

Ancient.

The red handprint fades to pale pink.

Then disappears entirely.

Rowan removes her hand.

"She will remember coming home from school," says Rowan, evenly. "Homework. Bed."

Izzy swallows, watching Rowan differently now.

"And the rest?"

"Will not follow her."

Rowan rises slowly.

Her eyes move back to Alaric.

Cold.

Measured.

"You accelerated this."

"She would have taken the child," he replies.

"And now Mara knows you chose."

He does not answer.

He doesn't need to.

The room feels heavier, the air tighter.

Rowan's gaze lingers on him a moment longer.

Then she says quietly:

"This was a test."

It hangs there.

Below, deep within stone and shadow—

An iron bowl fractures cleanly down the center.

Dark water spills across cold rock.

Mara looks down at the burned thread in her fingers.

Smoke curls from it.

Her jaw tightens.

"Alaric."

Not calm.

Not distant.

Furious.

The flame in the chamber bends sideways.

He chose.

He will answer for it.

Chapter
- 30 -
Crossing Lines

ose sleeps upstairs.

Spell bags in place.

The house feels different.

Not safe.

Fortified.

Rowan stands at the kitchen table.

Alaric remains near the back door.

Not leaving.

Not approaching.

Lily sits upright in a chair; hands folded in her lap.

Watching everything.

Izzy stands between them all.

And no one pretends this is small anymore.

Rowan breaks the silence.

"This was a test."

The words settle like iron.

"Mara suspected your reports," says Rowan, to Alaric. "Tonight, she confirmed it."

"She would have taken my daughter," says Izzy, evenly.

Rowan's eyes shift to her.

"Yes."

"And he stopped her."

A beat.

Rowan studies Izzy carefully.

"You think that absolves him?"

"I think it matters."

Alaric does not speak.

He lets Izzy stand in it.

Rowan notices.

"You chose," Rowan says to him.

"Yes."

No hesitation.

No apology.

Just fact.

"And you cannot return."

"I am aware."

The front door opens without a knock.

Maddie steps inside, a bottle of wine poking from her purse.

"Rowan texted 'Izzy's. Now.' I assume this isn't about wine?"

Her eyes land on Alaric.

"Oh. So, we're past pretending."

Rowan's gaze cuts to her.

"You knew."

Maddie stills.

"Knew what?"

"You suspected and said nothing."

Maddie exhales slowly.

"You would have shut it down."

Rowan does not deny it.

That says enough.

Lily speaks softly from the table.

"She didn't care that Rose doesn't have powers."

Everyone looks at her.

"She wasn't supposed to be touched. That didn't matter."

Her jaw tightens.

"We can't pretend this is contained."

Rowan looks at Lily differently now.

Not as a child.

"As of tonight," Rowan says, "we stop pretending."

Her gaze returns to Alaric.

"You will not move freely in this house."

He nods once.

"You will not give orders."

Another nod.

"You will not involve the children."

His jaw tightens slightly.

"Yes."

Izzy's voice is steady when she says:

"He stays."

It is not a request.

Rowan looks at her.

Long.

Measuring.

"I'm not blind," says Rowan, calmly. "I feel the connection between you."

Silence.

Izzy doesn't look away.

"I'm not sending him back to be executed."

Alaric's expression shifts, just slightly.

Rowan exhales.

"We will call a meeting. Inner circle only. Boundaries will be drawn."

Her eyes flick between Izzy and Alaric.

"And if this continues, it will be deliberate."

No illusion.

No denial.

War requires clarity.

After a moment, Rowan turns to Izzy.

"Walk me out."

The porch is quiet.

The night thick.

Rowan stops at the steps.

"You do not get to be reckless now," she says.

"I'm not."

"You are emotionally compromised."

"I know."

Rowan studies her.

"If you lose focus, people die."

The words are not cruel.

They are true.

"I won't lose focus," Izzy says.

Rowan searches her face one last time.

"Then prove it."

She leaves without another word.

Inside, Maddie squeezes Izzy's hand once before heading for the door.

"Text me if he grows horns or some more weird shit happens," she says.

The door shuts behind her.

Lily lingers near the stairs.

"You're not sending him away?" she asks.

"No."

Lily nods once.

Then she steps a little closer, lowering her voice.

"He nodded at me."

Izzy looks at her.

"Like … he approved," adds Lily, softer now. "Like I did it right."

Izzy's expression softens.

"Yeah," she says gently. "You did."

She pulls Lily into a brief hug.

Not dramatic.

Just solid.

"I'm proud of you," says Izzy, against her hair.

Lily straightens slightly at that.

Then she heads upstairs.

The house goes still.

Finally.

Alaric remains near the back door.

Still.

Controlled.

Waiting.

Izzy walks toward him slowly.

"You can't go back," she says.

"No."

"And you knew that when you did it."

"Yes."

Silence settles between them.

Not tense.

Heavy.

"You didn't hesitate," she says.

"I did."

She looks up at him.

"When?"

"When I handed her the blade."

She understands.

He chose.

Fully.

The weight of that hits differently now.

"You don't have to stand by the door," she says.

He steps forward instead.

Not invading.

Not claiming.

Just closer.

His arms wrap around her.

Not urgent.

Not hungry.

Just solid.

She exhales into his chest.

Her body relaxes.

His hand rests at the back of her head.

Protective.

Not possessive.

"She will not be touched again," he says.

It isn't a promise he can guarantee.

But it's one he intends to keep.

She nods against him.

They stand like that for a long moment.

The war has begun.

But tonight—

He stays.

Chapter
- 31 -
Surrender

The house is quiet.

Rose is still asleep.

Lily's light is finally off.

The television glows softly in the living room, muted.

Alaric sits on the couch like he has every night since he arrived.

Boots off.

Shirt sleeves rolled.

Guarded even at rest.

He has not once assumed he belonged in her bed.

Izzy stands at the hallway entrance watching him.

For a moment she just takes him in.

This man who chose her.

Who chose her daughters.

Who chose exile.

He senses her before she speaks.

His eyes lift.

Soft.

Questioning.

She walks toward him slowly.

No rush.

No fear.

She stops in front of him.

Reaches down.

Takes his hand.

"Come to bed with me," she whispers.

No coyness.

No hesitation.

Just truth.

His jaw tightens— not resistance, but restraint snapping thin.

"You are certain?" he asks quietly.

She leans down, her lips brushing the edge of his ear.

"I'm not asking twice."

That does it.

He stands.

Follows her.

In the bedroom, the door closes behind them.

Not slammed.

Not urgent.

Deliberate.

For a moment they just stand there facing each other.

The air feels different.

He steps closer first.

Slower than before.

Measured.

But his hands are not hesitant.

They slide around her waist, pulling her against him.

She exhales— warmth spreading through her body like something long denied finally answered.

Relief.

He kisses her like he's been holding back for days.

Not frantic.

Deep.

Claiming.

Certain.

Her hands move to his shoulders, then into his hair.

She doesn't pull away.

She doesn't hold back.

She doesn't deflect.

She lets herself want him.

He breaks the kiss only long enough to look at her.

Really look at her.

No shadows.

No war.

No strategy.

Just her.

"You are extraordinary," he says.

Her throat tightens.

She reaches for the buttons on his shirt.

His hands move beneath the hem of hers, lifting it slowly, deliberately— not rushed, not stolen.

Chosen.

Fabric falls to the floor.

His mouth traces the line of her neck; then lower, reverent and certain.

Her breath breaks when his hands find her hips and pull her closer.

She reaches for his belt, but before she can finish, he lifts her effortlessly and lays her back against the sheets.

The rest unfolds without restraint.

Without apology.

Clothes forgotten on the floor.

Skin against skin.

Breath tangled.

Years of loneliness dissolved under steady hands and whispered promises.

He does not rush her.

He does not treat her like something fragile.

He moves with her— matching her rhythm, answering her.

When she pulls him closer, he doesn't hold back.

When he finally sinks into her, it is not hurried.

It's inevitable.

Her back arches.

A moan leaves her lips— not quiet, not careful.

Satisfied.

They move together like the war does not exist.

Like time does not exist.

Like this was always meant to happen.

Later—

They lie tangled together in sheets that smell like her.

The house silent.

The war distant for a few stolen hours.

His fingers trace slow patterns along her skin.

"You should have sent me away," he murmurs.

She shifts, propping herself slightly over him.

"And miss this?"

A faint smile touches his mouth.

"You are dangerous."

"I've been told."

His expression softens.

"You deserve peace."

She studies him.

"For the first time in a long time," she says, "I don't feel like I'm bracing for impact."

He pulls her closer.

She falls asleep against him, the steady rhythm of his heartbeat beneath her ear.

Below—

Mara waits.

Chapter
- 32 -
Exile

he first thing I learn about having a man from Below living in my house is this:

He doesn't sleep.

Not like we do.

He rests in phases— sitting upright on the couch with his arms folded like the world might try something stupid while he blinks.

Which is… unsettling.

And weirdly comforting.

The second thing I learn is that Rose has absolutely no fear of him.

Not a shred.

Rose comes downstairs in an oversized hoodie and slides to a stop when she sees him on the couch.

Her gaze rakes over him like she's reviewing a potential new stepdad in a catalog.

"Okay," she says, slowly. "So… you're still here."

Alaric looks up.

Calm. Polite. Controlled.

"Yes," he says. "I hope that's okay."

Rose nods as if that's perfectly reasonable.

"Cool. Do you eat food? Or do you, like… absorb moonlight and vibes?"

Lily freezes by the kitchen entrance.

Because Lily knows what he is.

Rose does not.

And I'm still trying to figure out how to keep it that way without lying so hard my ancestors haunt me.

Alaric answers without blinking. "I eat."

Rose looks disappointed. "Damn."

"Language," I snap automatically.

She glances at me like the word was necessary in that moment.

I set a plate of scrambled eggs on the counter and shoot her a warning look.

She grins. "What? I'm just asking questions."

Alaric stands and moves into the kitchen carefully— like he still doesn't trust he's allowed to be fully himself in my home.

Rose watches him like she's memorizing his posture.

Then she leans toward me and whispers, loudly,

"Mom, is he your boyfriend?"

My whole body locks.

Lily's head snaps up, and a small giggle escapes before she can stop it. She immediately ducks her head back down to her breakfast.

Alaric pauses mid-step.

I clear my throat. "Rose."

"What?" she says, innocently. "I'm not judging. I'm just… observing."

I glance at Alaric.

His face is still neutral.

But his jaw tightens— just slightly.

And I hate how much I notice that now.

"He's… a friend," I say, carefully.

Rose hums like she doesn't believe me for a second.

Lily moves past us and reaches for a cup, focused on not reacting again.

As Alaric passes her chair, he rests his hand lightly on the back of it.

Not touching her.

Just there.

A quiet shield.

Lily's shoulders drop a fraction.

She doesn't look at him.

But she exhales.

I see it.

I see all of it.

And something inside me shifts again— not fear this time.

Something that feels like belonging.

Later, when the girls are at school and the house is quiet, I find Alaric standing at the kitchen window.

He's watching the road like he's expecting something to come screaming up the driveway.

"Do you miss it?" I ask.

He doesn't turn. "Below?"

"Yes."

A pause.

Then, blunt as truth.

"I miss nothing that lacks choice."

Because exile is one thing.

But choice?

Choice changes everything.

I step closer. "If this is exile…"

His head tilts slightly, as though he's weighing the word.

Then he turns fully.

Without warning, his hand hooks into the front of my jeans and pulls me into him.

It isn't rough.

It's certain.

And there—just for a second—something human breaks through his control.

"If this is exile," he says, "I accept it."

My throat tightens.

I wrap my arms around his waist and look up into his deep blue eyes.

"For now," I say softly, "I'm going to soak in what's good."

His gaze holds mine a beat longer than necessary.

Then his eyes shift past me toward the hallway— reminding himself where he is.

What's at stake.

The war we haven't seen yet.

But for now—

we just stand silently in the light.

Chapter
- 33 -
Target

y day three, it's obvious we can't keep pretending this is temporary.

Alaric has one outfit.

One.

And I'm not judging—he literally got stranded in my world—but I'm also not letting Rose walk around telling people my "friend" wears the same shirt every day like a haunted cowboy.

So, I do what any reasonable woman does when reality becomes too weird to process:

I take my family to Target.

We walk in, and Alaric stops dead in the entryway like he's hit an invisible wall.

Automatic doors. Fluorescent lights. Rows of humans.

A wall of seasonal décor screaming SPRING like it's a threat.

His eyes track everything at once.

Not fear.

Assessment.

Rose nudges him. "You okay, Al?"

Alaric's head turns slowly. "Do not call me that if you expect me to answer."

Rose bursts out laughing.

Lily covers her mouth with her sleeve, barely containing her own smile.

I try not to grin.

Fail.

We make it to men's clothing.

I toss shirts into the cart. Jeans. Socks. A jacket.

Rose holds up a graphic tee and squints. "This one says 'Weekend Mode.' That feels … wrong for him."

Lily picks up a plain black shirt and hands it to me without a word.

Practical. Serious. Lily.

I glance at Alaric. "Try these."

He looks at the dressing rooms like they're a trap.

Rose points. "It's just a tiny room. No one fights you in there."

Alaric's eyes narrow slightly. "People fight you in rooms here?"

Rose blinks. "No, silly. You go in there to try on clothes."

He considers that.

Then goes in.

He comes out five minutes later wearing a fitted black shirt that makes him look unfairly normal.

Like he belongs in my world.

Like he could've always been here.

Like he's not a blade wearing a man's face.

Rose stares at him and nods once. "Okay. Damn."

I elbow her. "Rose."

"What? I said 'okay.'"

Lily's gaze flicks to him— quickly and privately. She gives the smallest nod of approval.

Then looks away again

We keep walking.

We pass Starbucks.

Rose points. "That. We're doing that."

Alaric watches the barista like she's performing sorcery.

When Rose hands him a smoothie, he holds it cautiously, as if it might bite him.

He takes one sip.

Freezes.

Then takes another.

Slower.

His eyes lift to me.

"This is … cold."

I blink. "Yes."

He studies the cup like it's personally offensive. "And sweet."

"Yes."

Lily laughs softly. "He's having an existential crisis over a strawberry smoothie."

Alaric doesn't deny it.

Lily sips hers and murmurs, almost to herself, "It's kind of cute."

I pretend I didn't hear that.

But my chest warms anyway.

We end up in the snack aisle.

Rose tosses Takis into the cart.

Lily adds fruit snacks.

Alaric picks up a box of Pop-Tarts and reads the label like it's a spell.

He looks at me. "These are … for breakfast?"

"Sometimes," I say.

His eyes narrow.

"You feed children sugar for breakfast."

"Welcome to America," says Rose, brightly.

Alaric exhales like he's trying not to laugh.

And then he does.

Not loud.

Not big.

Just a surprised sound— like it slipped out before he could stop it.

Rose's eyes widen. "Oh my God. He laughed."

Alaric's expression resets instantly.

Rose points at Lily. "Did you see that?"

Lily nods once. "Yes."

Then she looks at him with faint satisfaction.

Like she just witnessed proof he's not made entirely of sharp edges.

On the drive home, Alaric sits in the passenger seat, watching traffic like it's a living organism.

"This world is loud," he says.

I keep my eyes on the road. "Yeah."

A pause.

Then, quieter—

"But it is … light."

My hands tighten on the steering wheel.

Because that's what I want.

For him to feel it.

To want it.

To choose it.

And not just because he can't go back.

Chapter
- 34 -
Black

ose paints his nails on a Thursday night.

It happens the way most disorder occurs in my house— casual, unplanned, and somehow inevitable.

I walk into the living room and stop.

Rose is sitting cross-legged on the rug with a bottle of black nail polish.

Alaric is in a dining chair pulled into the center of the room like he's being questioned by authorities.

His hands are extended.

Very still.

Very patient.

Lily sits on the couch with her journal open, pretending she isn't watching like this is the most important thing she's seen all week.

"Rose," I say, slowly.

Rose doesn't look up. "He agreed."

Alaric's eyes lift to mine.

"I agreed," he confirms.

"Why?" I ask.

Rose finally looks up and grins. "Because black suits him."

Lily murmurs without looking up, "It does."

Alaric's jaw tightens slightly.

I point at him. "You do that thing with your jaw when you're unsettled."

"I am not unsettled," he replies calmly.

Rose paints another nail with the focus of a surgeon.

"You're totally unsettled," she says.

He does not argue.

Because he knows better than to argue with a teenage girl "holding chemicals."

When she finishes, she lifts his hand like she's presenting evidence.

"There," she says proudly. "See? Hot."

"Rose," I warn automatically.

"What? It's a compliment."

Alaric studies his hand.

The black polish against his skin looks … intentional.

Strangely fitting.

"Is this permanent?" he asks.

"No," says Rose, brightly. "Unless you commit to it."

He nods once. "Acceptable."

Rose throws her head back laughing. "Acceptable! I'll take it."

Lily's shoulders shake with quiet laughter.

And then—

It happens.

Alaric smiles.

Not the restrained half-curve he allows in public.

A real one.

Small.

Unfiltered.

Rose gasps like she just witnessed a solar eclipse.

"Mom! He smiled!"

"I saw," I say, unable to hide my own.

The house feels warm.

Easy.

For a moment, war feels far away.

Later, the girls head upstairs.

Rose yells goodnight and disappears.

Lily lingers an extra second before climbing the steps, like she doesn't fully trust the quiet yet.

When their doors shut, the house settles.

Alaric stands at the kitchen counter; hands braced lightly against the edge.

Watching the windows.

The back door.

The dark.

I lean against the opposite side of the counter.

"You're thinking," I say.

"Yes."

"About?"

"Mara."

The name shifts the air immediately.

"She will not leave us unobserved," he continues. "She will send watchers."

"More than one?"

"Possibly many."

My chest tightens.

"They will test boundaries," he says. "Follow you. Follow the girls."

The girls.

"Especially Rose," he adds.

That hits harder than anything else tonight.

My stomach drops.

"Why Rose?"

"She is untrained," he says, quietly. "Lily can defend herself to a degree. Rose cannot. Not yet."

Fear moves through me fast and sharp.

I straighten.

"No one touches her."

He says it first.

And he says it like a vow.

His eyes meet mine.

"I will not allow it."

"But you can't be everywhere," I snap, the fear leaking through.

His voice remains level. "I will guard them."

"Both of them?"

"Yes."

Silence stretches between us.

Then—

"If Mara comes Above," he says, calmly, "I will meet her face to face."

The certainty in his voice makes my pulse spike.

"That's not a plan," I say.

"It is part of one."

I fold my arms across my chest.

"Okay. Then what's the rest of it?"

"We build layers," he says. "You stay connected to Rowan. Maddie as well. You are still learning. You do not know every protection."

I don't like hearing that.

But it's true.

"I don't want to put more on them," I say.

"You are not putting anything on them," he replies. "They are already in this."

That settles something in me.

He steps closer— not invading, not heated.

Focused.

He takes both of my hands in his.

Looks me directly in the eyes.

Grounding.

"We prepare, we call a meeting with Rowan and Maddie," he says. "We do not react."

"Meaning?"

"Wards reinforced. Movement watched. Patterns altered. You do not travel alone if avoidable. The girls are not left unattended."

I exhale slowly.

"This was supposed to be normal," I yell!

His gaze softens slightly.

"It can be," he says. "But we protect it."

I look toward the hallway where the girls sleep.

Rose with black nail polish still smudged on her thumb.

Lily pretending she isn't listening to everything.

I turn back to him.

"Then we prepare," I say.

He nods once.

Deliberate.

Not afraid.

Just ready.

Now I understand something clearly:

This isn't about surviving her.

It's about defending what we've built.

Chapter
- 35 -
In the Dark

 wake in the dark.

No sound.

No reason.

Just a feeling.

The air is wrong.

Heavy.

I turn over.

And stop breathing.

Alaric is on his back beside me.

Eyes open.

Unblinking.

His throat is cut clean across.

Blood soaks the pillow beneath him. It has spread into the sheets, dark and thick, reaching toward my side of the bed.

For a moment, I don't understand what I'm seeing.

My brain refuses to translate it.

Then the metallic smell hits.

Sharp.

Real.

"No," I whisper.

I reach for him.

His skin is cold.

Too cold.

My fingers come away wet.

I jerk back.

"No. No, no—"

He doesn't move.

Doesn't blink.

Doesn't breathe.

The mark on my hand burns suddenly.

Hot.

Bright beneath my skin.

I scramble out of bed.

"Rose!"

No answer.

I run to her room and shove the door open.

Her bed is empty.

The covers thrown back.

Her pillow on the floor.

"Lily!"

Down the hall.

Her room.

Empty.

Window closed.

Closet door open.

No Lily.

My pulse pounds so hard I can barely hear.

I run downstairs.

Bare feet slamming against wood.

The kitchen lights are on.

Everything looks normal.

Except—

The air near the center of the room shimmers.

A thin vertical slit hangs in space.

Exactly like the night Esther came.

Not wide.

Not fully open.

Just … there.

Cold breath seeps from it.

I step closer.

My hands are shaking.

"Give them back," I whisper.

The slit hums faintly.

And then—

Nothing.

It seals.

The air goes still.

The house is silent.

Alaric is dead upstairs.

My daughters are gone.

The mark on my hand glows bright enough to see in the dark.

The room tilts.

I bolt upright in bed with a gasp that tears my throat raw.

Darkness.

No blood.

No seam.

I turn immediately.

Alaric is beside me.

Alive.

Breathing.

His eyes open instantly.

"Isobel."

My hand flies to his throat.

Whole.

Warm.

I choke on a sob.

"You were—" I can't finish.

"It was a dream," he says, quietly.

"No," I whisper. "It wasn't just a dream."

The mark on my hand glows faintly between us.

He sees it.

His jaw tightens.

"She reached you."

"Mara."

He nods once.

"She killed you," I say. "The girls were gone. There was a slit in the kitchen."

He takes my wrist gently.

"She cannot physically harm anyone in their sleep," he says. "But she can fracture you."

"She's trying to break me."

"Yes."

My breathing is still uneven.

He studies me for a second.

"I need you to show me," he says.

He grips my forearm.

"Close your eyes. Think of it."

I don't want to.

But I do.

I close my eyes.

The bed.

The blood.

The empty rooms.

The slit in the kitchen.

His body cold under my hand.

His grip tightens.

Sharp.

When I open my eyes, his face is controlled.

But colder.

"She is testing your threshold," he says.

"To see what?"

"How much you can endure before you unravel."

I pull my hand back.

"I won't unravel."

"I know."

Silence.

Then—

"I'm calling Rowan."

"Yes."

No hesitation.

No argument.

"We prepare," he says.

I grab my phone from the nightstand.

My hands are still shaking when Rowan answers.

"What happened?"

"Mara," I say. "She came into my dream. Alaric's throat was cut. The girls were gone. There was a slit in the kitchen."

A beat of silence.

Then Rowan's voice hardens.

"Tell me everything."

Alaric sits upright beside me.

Watching the room.

Listening.

Guarding.

The mark on my hand still glows faintly in the dark.

And somewhere Below—

I know she felt that, too

Chapter
- 36 -
The Gathering

It's close to midnight when we pull into Rowan's driveway.

The house is lit.

Not warmly.

Intentionally.

Alaric steps out first.

Lily follows.

I lock the car; my pulse still unsettled from the dream.

Rose is safe at a sleepover.

Normal.

Laughing somewhere.

I repeat that to myself as we walk toward the door.

Rowan opens it before we knock.

She doesn't greet us.

She steps aside.

"Come in."

The air inside is different.

Dense.

Focused.

The living room is full.

Not six women.

Not the usual circle.

At least twenty.

Maybe more.

Different ages.

Different faces.

All quiet.

All watching.

The sound of the door shutting behind us echoes louder than it should.

For a moment, I feel like I've stepped into something I was never meant to see.

Alaric remains near my shoulder.

Not hiding.

Not forward.

Present.

Maddie crosses the room first.

She squeezes my hand once.

"You look like hell," she says.

"Thanks."

Rowan steps into the center of the room.

No theatrics.

No raised voice.

But the room settles instantly around her.

"She entered Isobel's dream."

The words drop into silence.

Murmurs ripple softly through the room.

"She killed him," I say. "In the dream."

Every eye shifts briefly to Alaric.

He doesn't react.

"She took the girls," I add. "There was a seam in the kitchen."

Silence follows that.

Not disbelief.

Assessment.

Rowan nods once.

"This confirms escalation."

She moves toward the table where a long, iron-wrapped object rests.

Wrapped carefully.

Deliberately.

"The Veilblade," she says.

The cloth is pulled back just enough to reveal the matte metal.

Even in a room full of witches, it feels wrong.

"There is only one," Rowan continues. "Mara possessed it. She gave it to Esther."

Her gaze shifts briefly to Alaric.

"Esther is dead."

No one questions that.

"Without this blade," Rowan continues, "no witch Below can open a seam."

A woman near the fireplace speaks softly. "Unless she comes herself."

"She will not," replies Rowan, calmly. "Not without certainty."

The room goes quiet again.

I step forward before I can stop myself.

"What does this mean?"

Rowan looks directly at me.

"It means we seal the threshold."

The words are almost more unreal than the dream.

Maddie exhales slowly.

A few of the older women nod like they've been expecting this.

"If we seal it," Rowan continues, "no crossing. No watchers. No interference from Below."

"For how long?" I ask.

"Until Mara dies."

There it is.

Blunt.

Clean.

"She is aging," Rowan says. "Her health is not strong. Time is not on her side."

"But until then," Maddie adds quietly, "we make sure she cannot reach you."

Lily shifts beside me.

I glance down.

She isn't afraid.

She's listening.

Absorbing.

One of the older women studies her openly.

"The younger one has strength," she says.

Lily meets her gaze without flinching.

Rowan notices.

"Lily will stand in the circle when we seal it."

My stomach tightens.

"She's fifteen."

"She is part of this," replies Rowan, evenly.

Lily doesn't argue.

She nods once.

Alaric finally speaks.

"If you seal it, you must understand what that means."

All eyes shift to him.

"You cut Below off entirely," he continues. "No passage. No messages. No correction."

Rowan's expression doesn't change.

"Yes."

He holds her gaze.

"If it is sealed, I do not return."

The room stills.

Rowan studies him for a long moment.

"You chose," she says.

"Yes."

Not dramatic.

Not loud.

Just truth.

I feel it in my chest.

Rowan turns back to the room.

"We combine power," she says. "All of us. We anchor from this side. We close the seam completely."

"When?" someone asks.

Rowan looks at me.

"Soon."

"How soon?" I press.

"Before she makes the next move."

The words settle heavy in the room.

Because we all know what that means.

If Mara senses the sealing—

She will come to stop it.

I swallow.

Rose is at a sleepover.

Normal.

Unaware.

And I suddenly understand something very clearly.

This is no longer about reacting.

This is about forcing an end.

Rowan pulls the cloth back over the Veilblade.

"We gather again tomorrow night," she says. "Full circle. No hesitation."

The women begin to disperse slowly.

Not frightened.

Not scattered.

Prepared.

Alaric leans closer to me, voice low.

"She will feel this."

"I know."

His hand brushes mine.

The mark beneath my skin flickers faintly.

Let her feel it.

Since the dream—

I am not afraid.

I am ready.

Chapter
- 37 -
Fracture

owan's house smells like iron and smoke.

The furniture has been pushed back.

The rug rolled away.

Salt lines the floor in a wide circle, thick and deliberate. Iron filings dust the outer edge like a warning.

Candles burn at even intervals.

Not decorative.

Functional.

The coven stands shoulder to shoulder around the perimeter.

Twenty women.

Maybe more.

No one speaks above a whisper.

Lily stands at my right.

Her chin is lifted.

She is pale.

But steady.

Rowan moves through the circle one final time, checking placements.

"Once we begin," she says calmly, "no one breaks formation. No one steps out unless I say."

Her eyes land on me.

"You anchor."

I nod.

My mark is already warm.

Alaric stands outside the circle near the back wall.

Not excluded.

Guarding.

His attention is not on us.

It's on the air.

On the unseen.

Maddie hands Rowan the iron-wrapped bundle.

The Veilblade.

Rowan does not unwrap it.

She sets it in the center of the circle.

Not as a weapon.

As a relic.

As proof.

"There is only one threshold," Rowan says. "We seal it from here."

The room stills further.

Rowan lifts her hands.

The women follow.

I do the same.

Lily mirrors me without hesitation.

The first chant is low.

Not dramatic.

Not loud.

Ancient words that feel older than language.

The air shifts.

Not violently.

Subtly.

Like pressure building behind glass.

The salt trembles faintly.

The candles bend inward.

My mark flares hot.

I gasp before I can stop it.

"Stay anchored," says Rowan, calmly.

I close my eyes.

I picture the seam.

The place where the air tears.

I picture it stitching shut.

Sealing.

Closing.

The chanting deepens.

Voices layer.

Twenty rhythms become one.

The floor vibrates faintly beneath my bare feet.

Lily's fingers brush mine.

Not afraid.

Connected.

Outside the circle, Alaric stiffens.

His head tilts slightly.

"She feels it," he says, quietly.

Rowan does not break cadence.

"Continue."

The temperature drops.

Not like winter.

Like shadow.

The candles flicker violently.

The iron filings along the circle lift slightly— hovering.

My mark burns brighter.

Pain lances up my arm.

I grit my teeth.

The air in the center of the circle tightens.

Compresses.

Like something pushing back from the other side.

A faint vertical shimmer appears in the center of the room.

Not fully formed.

Just … strain.

The chanting intensifies.

The shimmer deepens.

The house groans.

Lily's breath catches.

"Hold," Rowan commands.

The shimmer widens a fraction.

Cold air spills into the room.

Not a seam.

Not yet.

But close.

Alaric steps forward instinctively.

Rowan snaps without looking at him, "Do not enter the circle."

He stops.

The pressure spikes.

The shimmer pulses.

And somewhere Below—

Something pushes back.

The salt line cracks in one place.

Just a hairline fracture.

Rowan's voice sharpens.

"Reinforce."

The coven's voices rise.

Power slams inward toward the center.

The shimmer distorts violently.

For a heartbeat—

The air almost tears.

Then—

Darkness flickers behind it.

Not a form.

Not a face.

Just presence.

The house lights shatter.

Glass starts to rain down.

The salt line blows outward in a shockwave.

Candles extinguish all at once.

Silence crashes into the room.

The shimmer collapses.

Gone.

The house is dark except for moonlight through broken windows.

No seam.

No opening.

Just the echo of what almost was.

Rowan lowers her hands slowly.

"She knows," says Alaric into the silence.

No one argues.

My mark still glows faintly beneath my skin.

But, not hot now.

Not painful.

Alive.

Rowan's voice is steady when she speaks.

"She will not wait."

The coven stands breathing in the dark.

And I understand something with absolute clarity—

We did not seal it.

We provoked her.

Chapter
- 38 -
The Threshold

The darkness in Rowan's house does not settle.

It waits.

The coven stands frozen in the wreckage.

Then—

The air in the center of the circle tears open.

A seam rips downward like fabric being split by force.

Cold floods the room.

Alaric steps forward instantly.

"Mara."

She steps through the threshold.

Thinner than I imagined.

Older.

But her eyes burn with feral clarity.

"You dare," she says softly.

Rowan's voice cuts through the room.

"Hold."

The coven tightens formation.

Mara's gaze sweeps the circle.

Then stops.

On Lily.

Of course.

"You stand in power too soon," says Mara, scolding.

Lily stiffens.

I feel it beside me.

Then Mara moves.

Faster than breath.

Her arm shoots through the fractured edge of the salt line and wraps around Lily's wrist.

Lily gasps.

The seam widens instantly.

Hungry.

Alaric lunges but Rowan shouts—

"Do not break the circle!"

Power is still anchoring.

If he steps in, it collapses.

Mara pulls.

Lily's feet slide across the floor toward the seam.

"Mom!"

The sound detonates something primal inside me.

The coven chants harder.

The seam flickers.

I don't think.

I break formation.

Rowan shouts my name.

Too late.

I step into the center of the circle.

Into the cold.

Into her.

Mara's eyes lock onto mine.

"You cannot keep what belongs Below."

My mark ignites.

Blinding hot.

I grab her arm.

Solid.

Real.

And I push.

Everything in me pushes.

Not magic.

Not words.

Force.

Alaric grabs Lily at the same time, and yanks her backward.

Mara stumbles toward the seam.

The coven's power slams inward.

The threshold begins to strain.

Mara claws forward, furious.

Her dress catches in the tightening seam.

Fabric tears violently.

She screams.

Not words.

Rage.

The seam snaps shut with a crack that shakes the house.

Silence detonates outward.

The salt line sucks inward this time, sealing.

Candles shatter.

The room goes still.

Lily collapses into Alaric's arms.

Alive.

Shaking.

The torn strip of Mara's dark gown lies smoking in the center of the floor.

Proof she was here.

Rowan rises slowly.

Breathing hard.

"It's sealed," she says.

No one cheers.

No one moves.

I kneel beside Lily.

She looks up at me.

Wide-eyed.

Not broken.

Just changed.

Alaric meets my gaze over her head.

The threshold is closed.

And this time—

It holds.

Chapter
- 39 -
Enough

The house is too quiet.

Not the waiting kind.

The finished kind.

Smoke curls faintly from the torn strip of fabric on the floor.

No one moves to touch it.

Lily is still in Alaric's arms.

Her fingers clutch his shirt.

He doesn't try to loosen her grip.

He just holds.

Izzy kneels in front of them.

Her hands are still shaking.

Rowan rises first.

She steps into the center of the ruined circle.

All eyes turn to her.

"The threshold is sealed," she says.

The room steadies.

"It will hold."

Silence follows.

"Mara is alive," says Rowan, plainly. "But she is contained."

No one argues.

No one panics.

They stand in that truth together.

Behind them, Lily slowly releases Alaric's shirt.

He looks down at her.

"You held," he says.

She nods once.

He helps her to her feet.

Izzy rises, too.

For a moment, the three of them face one another in the dim light.

"It's over?" Lily says.

Izzy kneels slightly so they're eye level.

"We're safe for now," she says, gently.

Lily looks between them.

"You didn't hesitate," she says.

Not to one of them.

To both.

Izzy shakes her head.

Alaric meets Lily's gaze and gives a quiet nod.

He steps closer to Izzy.

"In any world," he says, "I would choose this one."

Izzy exhales.

She kisses him.

Not rushed.

Not desperate.

Certain.

When they separate, Lily steps forward and wraps her arms around them.

Alaric's hand rests at the back of Lily's head.

Izzy's arms close around them.

Three bodies.

One line.

The torn strip of Mara's gown lies dark and silent behind them.

The threshold is sealed.

Mara is still alive.

But tonight—

They stand together.

And for now, that is enough.

www.ingramcontent.com/pod-product-compliance
Lightning Source LLC
LaVergne TN
LVHW090557110826
845146LV00001B/161

* 9 7 9 8 9 9 5 3 8 0 3 0 6 *